Megan's

Christmas Knight

Sue,
Happy Holidays!
Beth Warstadt

Megan's

Christmas Knight

Beth Warstadt

Gilded Dragonfly Books

ISBN: 978-1-943095-20-9

Cover Design: John Barfield/Gina Dyer

Photograph: Solomin Viktor/Depositphotos

Editor: Melba Moon, Mary Marvella

Interior Design: Melba Moon

Dedication

To those who still hear the bells of Christmas

And to Steve, Kevin, and Brian who give
everything meaning.

Chapter 1

The wind charged in like a freight train, whipping dried leaves into Meg's face with broad, open palms. What lunacy had driven her out to the weather-beaten cliffs of Cornwall in the path of a wild gale? Was it the madness of a woman trying to blast away memories stuck like barnacles to every waking dream and every sleeping nightmare? One jump, one quick leap, even an 'accidental' fall and it would all be over. Suicide was such a cowardly act, but if she simply relaxed her body, let all of her limbs go limp, the storm would surely take the blame and blow her out to sea. She would never again have to face her humiliation.

Because she was deafened by the roar of the wind, the horse and rider were on her without warning. The enormous beast reared up, threatening to crush her beneath its thrashing hooves. Her feet scrambling for balance, Meg found only emptiness above the deadly plunge to the sea. Just as she resigned herself to splattering on the rocks below, strong hands grabbed her and pulled her onto the solid earth. A clear masculine voice cut through the tumult as if there were no other sound.

"Come."

Scrambling to her feet, she surrendered to the stranger, taking his hand so he could pull her up onto the horse that had calmed with his touch. At full gait, he galloped toward the entrance to a cave screened from view by the glassy curtain of rain. They ducked together as they clambered through the passageway at full speed, coming to a sudden, violent halt when they were safe. The force of the stop propelled her into the back of her rescuer, whose strong hold on the horse prevented them both from flying off its back.

The hooded figure slipped off and lifted Meg down as easily as though she was a small child. Lightheaded and unsteady, she knew that this could not be happening. Could she dream if she was dead? Could she be hallucinating as the life drained out of her body where she had fallen onto the rocks? Only in romance novels and fantasy movies did women in distress get rescued by men on white horses. And those women deserved to be saved.

"Who are you?" she asked, panting, as he backed away from her, his hooded head bent to hide his face. He did not speak. "Please," she whispered. "Tell me who you are. Let me see your face."

A blinding flash and thunderous crack drew her attention out to the storm. She owed the mysterious stranger her life, but the hood and silence were too Ghost-of-Christmas-Future for her to let her guard down. Pushing aside her fears, she turned to speak to him again.

Man and horse were gone.

They had not ridden past her, had not made a noise behind her. Even with the deafening clamor of the storm they were too big, too solid to have disappeared without a sound, but disappear they had.

Meg swayed against the solid rock wall of the cave. It was cold and hard and *real.* She was definitely not in the place where she had started and had no other explanation how she'd gotten there, except the impossible truth. She had been rescued from gale force winds and pounding rain by a phantom on a ghost horse.

Phantom on a ghost horse?

She felt around the cave for a door or hidden passageway through which they might have disappeared. Her close inspection revealed that it wasn't a cave at all. The rocks were chiseled supports for some sort of storage cellar or storm shelter. The top was a ceiling supported by carefully placed lintels of hewn rock. All the sides were smooth, as though rubbed by hundreds of hands for hundreds of years. Moss and other darkness-seeking plants grew through the cracks, giving the man-made grotto a sense of immeasurable age.

Meg did not surrender her search until she noticed that the storm had blown itself out. Reluctantly she left her refuge and the mysterious dream hero. She had a long walk to her car and a long time to puzzle over the events of the last hour.

When she arrived back at the bed and breakfast its anxious owner grabbed her in a warm hug. "Thank goodness you're safe!" exclaimed Mrs. Bennett breathlessly. "We've been so worried about you. These storms can come up with no warning and blow a body out to sea so as we'd never know what happened. We didn't want to lose our first American guest without a trace."

Meg calmed her host with a comforting hand. "I'm fine. I rode it out in some sort of cave."

The motherly woman nodded wisely. "You found our fogou."

"Your what?"

"Our fogou. We're not sure as to where it came from, but it's so old no one knows anything about who put it there or why." She leaned in to share an intimate secret. "There's some say it's haunted."

"No kidding?" Meg forced her voice to sound casual.

Mrs. Bennett dropped her voice even lower, "There's some say they've seen a hooded figure on a ghost horse charge out of the fogou and ride off to God-knows-where, then vanish back inside through solid stone walls."

"Is that right?"

"You've seen him, haven't you?" The kind woman's demeanor changed. She stepped away as though Meg had brought a deadly contagion into her house. "They say his appearance is a bad sign. Some say he rides out for the Devil, searching for souls."

Meg was not usually superstitious, but she could not deny the aura of the supernatural she'd felt with him. He hadn't brought death to her, but life. "Are there more stories about him? What do they say about who he is or his connection to the fogou?"

"Well," Mrs. Bennett relaxed a little, enjoying the telling of the tale but being careful not to touch Megan, just in case. "This village has been here over a thousand years, and people say he was already here when they came. Some say he's a wild heathen that got left behind when they all went to Ireland. Others think he's a leftover Roman or a Druid or some such."

"What do you think?"

"Me? I think he's a leftover knight from King Arthur. The castle's not far from here."

"Tintagel."

"That's right. Have you been?"

"Not yet." Sightseeing had not been part of Megan's escape plan.

"Oh, my dear, how could you come here and not see Camelot? It's the reason people visit us."

Planning her trip to Tintagel for the next day, Meg spent the afternoon touring the village and collecting stories of the spectral rider. She found the population held quite a variety of opinions, though not one person doubted his existence. Many claimed they had seen him or knew someone who had, although always from a distance. No one she talked to had ever actually touched or spoken with him.

Some told her with a shudder that they believed he was Death, himself. Others believed the heathen priest theory, and still others subscribed to the Arthurian knight story. The owner of the local bookstore proposed the romantic scenario that he was a tortured soul haunting the wind-swept plains looking for his lost love, searching eternally for one who had died before he could make her his own.

"Does he have a name? Does he have a time?"

"Don't matter 't'all, does it now? True love is true love, don't matter the name or time."

The owner of the market had a different story. "There's times when people have a need and a bag of gold appears on their doorstep. Not only money, mind you, but gold coins, even in recent times." He spoke with a calm confidence the others had lacked. "First they thought it was leprechaun gold and it'd disappear soon as they tried to use it. Foolishness. There's no such thing as leprechauns. Nope, I say he's an angel of mercy sent by God when people have a deep need."

"An angel?"

He dismissed her suspicions with unshakeable faith. "Folks need clothes, they appear. Folks need food, it appears. Folks need money, it appears. No muss, no fuss, no by-your-leave."

"You're the first who's told me that. You seem awfully certain, to be the only one who believes it."

"I'm not the only one who believes it, but ghost stories are better for the tourists. Everybody knows that." He turned back to stocking his shelves.

Chapter 2

Through the night Meg's dreams were filled with a shadowy hero and a husky, soothing voice uttering, "Come." Dreams fresh on her mind and picnic lunch in hand, she left early for Camelot, hoping for some clue to the identity of her mysterious savior.

Tintagel rose out of the Cornish cliffs like stone pillars created by wind and water instead of the well-worn work of human hands. It stood watch over a vista of sapphire blue sea and gentle waves lapping at rocky beaches, with a rising tide that flooded Merlin's Cavern in the quiet cove below. Its ruined rooms and courtyards had become grassy patios for scenic stops, and long, steep, narrow bridges connected sites long ago separated by the incursions of the sea.

No question the place was haunted. Even in bright daylight Meg sensed shadowy figures strolling on the grounds. There were ladies in flowing gowns, lords in belted tunics, and knights in chain mail. Were they actually there or were they the hopeful product of a romantic imagination? Visible or not, there was no doubt ancient souls had never left its walls. Her rescuer, however, had been no transparent vapor or shadowy creation of an over-stimulated imagination. A strong, solid man had lifted her onto the back of a powerful white horse and whisked her away from danger. The memory of her arms around him and the synchronized rocking of their bodies on the animal's broad back made her lightheaded, and she looked for a place to sit down.

She rested against a pile of rubble that had once been a low stone wall. She could return to the site of the fogou, but she did not expect he would be there. Whatever had happened to her in the face of the deadly storm, her imagination had turned it into something it was not. Though she did believe in ghosts and other supernatural phenomena, she did not believe they would ever visit *her*, give *her* warnings, or save *her* from certain disaster. Maybe if she played the insanity card by claiming to have seen a ghost, those she left behind at home would forget her shameless display and the multiple worlds it had brought crashing down.

No. They would never forget.

As Meg drove back to the village her ego, so tenuously reassembled by the distraction of the horseman, splintered into the thousand shattered pieces that had driven her to her British escape. Regardless of whether her experience had been a supernatural phenomenon or a real rescue by a kind stranger, it did not erase the specters of scandal and humiliation that haunted her in the real world. Her life that had been was gone forever.

She slipped into the house, surreptitiously avoiding detection from her well-meaning hostess. She lay down on her bed and tried futilely to blank her mind. She hoped to drive out the visions of her transgressions and replace them with the hooded man in black, but they refused to be pushed aside. She could find no peace from the memory of enraged, devastated faces and livid voices. Finally she gave up and stole out as covertly as she had stolen in. There was only one place to go.

She went back to the windswept cliffs, back to where she now knew the ancient fogou lay silently concealed in the peaceful countryside, back to where

14

her adventure began. There was no storm today, no need for rescue. There were only her tortuous memories and the cliffs that offered their different kind of escape.

When horse and rider surprised her this time, they came without a whisper. She jumped at the warm hand on her shoulder and spun around to find him standing there, head still concealed under the black hood, leading the now serene white horse by reins he scarcely held. Her soul thrilled, but she couldn't tell if it was excitement or terror that set her heart pounding. When he reached up slowly to push back the hood her breath caught as she waited, wondering what was hidden underneath.

He was not a decaying, skeletal Ghost of Christmas Future. His face was young and handsome, and his blue eyes were at once merry and sad, as though he was glad to see her but knew the burdens of her heart. She could not tell his age because he had the enthusiasm and wonder of youth and the wisdom and serenity of old age.

He reached silently for her hand and led her away from the edge. They walked slowly, with the horse obediently following behind until distracted by a tasty clump of clover. She wanted desperately to hear him speak, but he remained silent and thoughtful. They walked across the sea plains until the setting sun lit the landscape in purples and pinks.

As they walked the tumult in her mind quieted. She should hold on to the guilt that she deserved, but it would not stick. Peace radiated from his warm hand up her arm and into her troubled heart.

Still he did not speak.

Could a ghost have warm hands? Could a phantom soothe her troubled soul? Could a handsome face mask the horrible countenance of a servant of evil? "Please," she pleaded, "please speak to me. Please let me hear your voice."

He didn't speak, didn't even look at her, but finally it didn't matter. Let him be a vengeful specter. Let him be a homicidal ghoul. Let him be an apparition of Death. For the first time in weeks she was at peace.

They came to the fogou, and she was reminded of standing at the door after a date. She looked up into his warm eyes and wondered if he would try to kiss her. He did not. Instead, he handed her a flower, a purple hyacinth.

She lifted it to her nose, closed her eyes, and inhaled deeply. She knew this sweet fragrance. It filled her mind with spring. When she opened her eyes man and horse were gone.

It was fully dark by the time she arrived at the bed and breakfast. Mrs. Bennett greeted her at the door.

"Dear, if you're going to keep disappearing, I'm going to turn to drink."

"I'm sorry."

"It's none of my business where you go or what you do, but when you take off like that, well, anything could happen to a woman alone."

"You're right, of course."

"Wherever did you get a hyacinth this time of year?" she asked, looking at the flower in Meg's hand.

"Out by the sea," Meg replied, looking away to hide the lie.

"Not in October. 'Twas our ghost, wasn't it?"

"What if I told you I got it at a florist in the village?"

"I'd say you're not a very good liar."

She was caught. "I guess not. Yes, I saw the rider out by the cliffs, and yes, he gave me this flower."

"You've done something you feel sorry for."

"Why do you say that?"

"Because the purple hyacinth is the flower of forgiveness. Whatever it is you feel bad for doing, he wants you to know you are forgiven."

"Why should he forgive me? I don't even know him."

"He's a ghost, dear. He doesn't have to make sense."

"Maybe not," Meg shook her head. "but I don't believe he is a ghost. His hand is warm to the touch. He feels solid enough, like a real man."

Her hostess pulled her apron over her mouth. "You let him touch you? Are you crazy? Don't let him touch you. He'll take you."

"I don't think he is Death, Mrs. Bennett. I saw his face today. He was young and handsome. I've never felt anything but kindness from him."

"Young and handsome, you say? What did he look like?" Mrs. Bennett asked.

"He has dark hair and blue eyes, Mrs. Bennett, and he looks to be no older than thirty. He is tall and strong and full of life."

"They say Satan is beautiful, you know, so as people will fall prey to him. Maybe he's just waiting to get you alone and snatch you away."

"Maybe so." She clenched and unclenched her hands by her side. This nosy woman had no invitation to ruin her fantasy with reason.

The change in Meg's demeanor was not lost on Mrs. Bennett, who smiled and shrugged. She dropped her apron. "I guess evil demons don't usually give flowers of forgiveness."

"Thank you." Meg knew her hostess meant well.

"I've left a plate for you on the stove. I didn't want you to miss my best roast beef and potatoes."

"You're kinder than I deserve, Mrs. Bennett. Thank you."

"I doubt that, dear. You're harder on yourself than you should be."

Harder than I should be? Meg sat down with her plate. There was no 'hard enough'. She looked at her gift from the mystery man. Surely he of the kind eyes did not realize the magnitude of her transgression..

She pushed the plate away and dropped her head on her hands. The faces returned, mocking, then horrified, then full of rage and, finally, distraught. Because of her. She could never run, she could never hide. Everywhere she went they followed her. She should trash the flower that offered an absolution that she would never know.

She couldn't will her hand to drop it into the waste bin. Instead, she took a glass from the cabinet and filled it with water. It would be the last thing she saw before sleep and the first when she woke up. Forgiveness. Did he know what the flower meant? Was that the intention of his choice? How could he know she needed to be pardoned? If he knew her crime, then he must also know that there was no pardon to be had.

Chapter 3

She tried to stop the dawn by keeping her eyes closed, but the bright sunlight shone through her eyelids like paper lanterns. Consciousness forced its way in. The nagging guilt arrived before the memory. She rolled over, opened her eyes, and there it was. Her life in ruins. The vividness of the visions told her she had become too well acquainted and comfortable with her surroundings. It was time to move on again. Time to find a new place with a new set of distractions to shift her focus for as long as possible.

Tears filled Mrs. Bennett's eyes when Megan told her she would be leaving. "It's been so nice to have another woman to talk to, if you take my meaning," she said, enveloping Megan with a motherly embrace. "And you have brought the most exciting adventure."

"Mrs. Bennett, if my little vacation is the most excitement you've had, then you need to get out more."

She chuckled and leaned in, saying confidentially, "I don't know, dear. The horseman has been here for a thousand years, and you're the first one I know who's actually seen his face and touched him. Don't know how long I'll have to wait before someone else is whisked away by a handsome ghost on a white horse." In an even lower voice she said, "Doesn't seem likely he's really a ghost, does it? Are you actually going to leave without finding out the truth?"

Meg sighed heavily. "I'm going out there now to take one more shot at solving the mystery. Truth is, real or not, the Wordless Horseman is part of a fantasy I don't deserve."

"You keep referring to your mistakes as though you killed someone." When Meg didn't offer the information she was hoping for, Mrs. Bennett shook her head. "Well, dear, whatever it is, I hope you're able to work it out. A young girl like you shouldn't be so sad and guilty all the time."

While her attention focused on seeing her phantom again, Meg's car seemed to drive itself to the fogou. She parked nearby. After a few minutes she got out and sat waiting, not sure what she should do.

She didn't have to wait long. Man and horse startled her when they appeared from the dark entrance like a dolphin breaking the surface of the sea. As soon as he saw her he pushed off his hood and graced her with a smile that turned her brain into melted chocolate. She knew she should be scared or at least careful, but his appearance and manner were so disarming that her common sense gave up the battle without a fight.

Heat flushed her whole body when he took her hand and kissed it, a gesture so old-fashioned and gallant that she would have doubted its sincerity from anyone else. He continued to hold her hand as they began their stroll across the plains. Still he did not speak.

As she relaxed, she became intensely aware of the life around her. She breathed deeply of the sea air and licked its salt off her lips. Gulls flew overhead, their cries plaintive and haunting. Tall grasses waved in the ocean breeze, and the air was tinged with a crisp fall chill. The sun warmed her face, and she closed her eyes, trusting him to lead her with sure steps. She did not open them until they stopped.

He had brought her to a scattered group of boulders where they could sit and look out at a lighthouse on its distant craggy cliff. The day was clear, the sea calm, but the structure maintained its lonely watch, sounding its foghorn and keeping its bright light burning, an ever-present sentinel warning seamen of the rocky waters below.

She watched the lighthouse, but he watched her. She could feel the intensity of his gaze as though it actually, physically touched her, reading the feelings of her heart and thoughts of her mind.

"You are leaving." The husky, soothing sound she had been longing to hear finally touched her.

"Yes," she answered.

"Don't."

"I have to."

He stood up silently, took her hand, and led her away from the rocks to the place where the horse grazed contentedly. As they neared, the animal raised its head. Immediately it shifted into a ready stance as its master climbed on.

"Good-bye," Meg said sadly.

He reached down to her, his sad expression reflecting her own. She took his hand and pressed it.

In one fell swoop he pulled her up behind him and took off.

The landscape blurred as they flew through it, the horse's hooves barely touching the ground. She found it difficult to focus, but one clear thought swam up into her mind. They were galloping toward the fogou.

Terrified, she saw the dark opening ahead and knew that this time they were not going to stop in the safety of the cellar. This was what she had been expecting. This was the true event she knew she deserved. He had waited until no one would be looking

21

for her and stolen her away, going she knew not where to a fate she could only guess.

She held tightly to the body of her kidnapper. They barreled inside and toward the rear with no change in speed. She braced herself for impact, but they passed through the solid rock wall without a micro-second's hesitation. The passage on the other side was the blackest darkness she had ever known. Though she could not see, she cowered from the low ceiling and walls so close they touched the ends of the hairs standing up on her arms. Horse and rider raced on with absolute confidence, as though they could either see in the dark or knew the tunnel so well that they had no fear of a misstep.

She wondered if the beautiful, angelic face of her kidnapper had transformed into the grotesque visage of a hellish demon. Where was he taking her? Would she ever see light again? Was this her punishment for her crime? For weeks she had felt with melancholy and self-loathing that she would burn in hell for what she had done, but now, with the possibility real, she changed her mind.

Of course, it was far more likely that he was merely a man, a stalker who had been watching for his chance and grabbed her to rape her senseless before he murdered her and left her dismembered body where no one could ever find it. Her parents would never know what had happened to her. Her nephews would grow up with her presence as only a shadowy vapor in their childhood memories. Would her co-workers and former friends, so viciously angry when she left them, have wished this end for her? Would they assume she had run away and be angrier, cursing her to the end she was about to face? Would they be worried, eventually remembering what they had once meant to each other and shared? In the darkness, in the frenzied movement of the rushing horse, in the midst of her terror and dread, her tears fell on the back of her captor for all that she had lost and would never know again.

Was it that in her terror time stretched out into eternity, or did they truly ride for hours in the darkness before she saw a light at the end of the tunnel? Instead of relief she wished for the darkness. This would be the place of her torture and murder, of unthinkable degradation, pain and horror. How would she handle the agony? Would she plead for mercy, offering to do anything he wanted so he wouldn't kill her? Would she beg for death in the face of hours of torture and pain?

They burst through the doorway and into the light. The horse immediately slowed and calmed, and the man in front of her relaxed. He threw his leg over and slid off the horse, then lifted her down next to him. She saw that it was the same beautiful face with the kind blue eyes that she had come to know. Her stomach unknotted. He did not look like a man who intended to throw her on the ground then rape and kill her. Her legs were weak, and he steadied her as he led her toward a nearby house.

When her eyes adjusted to the light, she saw that they had come to an English village not unlike the one she had left behind. The cottages and shops were all lit invitingly in the advancing twilight, though it had been morning when they began their mad dash from the sea. She shivered in the colder air, and he put his arm around her shoulders, pulling her close as they walked.

They passed the first house and a scattering more until they came to a building that was not only bigger on the bottom, but also had a second floor on top. It was the first on a street of shops, all with large picture windows casting squares of light on the well-worn path below.

They pushed through the door into a tavern. A boisterous, happy crowd filled the room, a tankard in every hand. Delicious smelling food filled every table. Children twirled and danced to the music of a roving fiddle-player, dodging here and there to avoid careless adult feet. The partiers interrupted their revelry briefly to raise their drinks in salute to her companion. He acknowledged them with a smile and a wave and led her to a quiet table in the corner.

The scent of freshly baked bread made her stomach grumble. A waitress arrived with two steins of amber liquid and a fresh-from-the-oven loaf on a wood cutting board. Her kidnapper cut a piece for her, which she ate with scant awareness of it in her hand. He watched her closely, reading the nuances of emotion play across her face, and then reached across the table and took her hand.

"Welcome to my home," he said softly.

She still felt shocked and disoriented. "You're not going to kill me?" The words tumbled from her mouth.

He chuckled. "No. I'm not going to kill you."

"No rape, no murder, no dismemberment?"

"Not at all."

She filled her lungs with a long, deep breath and slowly expelled it. She lifted the tankard, took a sip, and found it unlike anything she had ever tasted, both sweet and bitter, but delicious.

She regained her wits and took a more interested look at her surroundings. The revelers occasionally glanced their way, and one or two gave friendly nods, but they kept a respectful distance as she struggled to get her bearings.

When her scan of the crowd returned to the other occupant of her table, a new thought popped into her mind. "I don't even know your name."

"Nick," he replied. "My name is Nick."

"Nick what?"

"Just Nick."

"Nick." She let the sound roll out of her mouth on a breath. "What is this place?"

"It is a safe haven."

"Who are these people?"

"They are the people who live here."

A cryptic, evasive answer. "Why did you bring me here?"

"Because you need to be here."

Another dodge. "What? Why?"

"You will see when you are ready," he said patiently.

"What does that mean?"

"It means you have asked enough questions. Eat first and then you must sleep. There is a room for you upstairs."

Chapter 4

Meg slept more deeply than she had in a long, long time. She woke but did not open her eyes, determined to prolong her delicious repose in the cocoon of soft cotton sheets and woolen blankets. Visions of her race through the dark tunnel with Nick and the shocking discovery of the hidden village pushed into her consciousness. Had it all been a crazy dream? She rolled over and opened her eyes.

The cozy room was most definitely not the one she had rented from Mrs. Bennett, nor was it her room at home. The lace curtains parted just enough to give her a peek of the frosted window. Frosted? Was it winter? It had been fall when Nick spirited her away. How far had they come? A warm sweater and comfortable slacks, definitely not the clothes she had arrived in, lay carefully placed on the rocking chair next to the fireplace. A cheerful fire danced and crackled in the grate.

She found the clothes fit as though they had been made for her. She went cautiously down the stairs, anticipating lurking menace around every corner. The merry crowd had gone, but she heard activity in the kitchen and followed the sound. A round young woman hummed as she iced delicious looking cakes and cookies. Savory aromas wafted up from the bubbling pots on the stove.

The woman interrupted her work to pour hot water from the whistling kettle into a waiting teapot. "Come and have your tea," she said, smiling. "I'll wager you could use a soothing drink right about now."

"Yes, thank you." Meg accepted the steaming cup.

The young woman raised her voice and called out cheerfully, "Bobby!"

A boy of about eight came bounding in from the other room and slid across the kitchen floor as though it was a sheet of ice. "I'm here!"

"Run and tell Nick that Megan is awake."

He tore out the door like she had asked him to go and find Santa Claus.

Meg sat at the little kitchen table, and the friendly young woman sat across from her, pouring their tea. She set down a plate of cookies for them to share. "Megan, I'm Molly," she said in a happy voice, "I'm so glad to see you. I thought you would never wake up."

Disoriented by the unfamiliar surroundings and the woman she had never met who was speaking to her like an old friend, she asked, "Why? What time is it?"

"Two or so."

"How long did I sleep?"

"Two days."

That wasn't possible. "Two days? I don't think so. Why would you say such a thing?"

"Because it's true," Molly said patiently. "Nick told us you would be tired. He said to let you sleep until you woke up on your own."

"What else did he tell you?"

"Nothing. I'm guessing you've noticed he's a man of few words." She was not at all offended by Meg's hostile reaction. "Be calm, Meg. I'm not going to ask. You are my guest, and Nick has said you are worthy of my friendship. That is all I need to know."

Meg was disarmed by Molly's sincerity, and she felt compelled to be a more gracious guest, until she remembered how she had come to be there. "Wait a minute. Nick said I was worthy of your friendship? He kidnapped me!" She jumped up and began to pace frantically around the kitchen.

"He took you to save you. He brings people here to help them when they are most desperate. You must have been in a very bad way."

Her voice was comforting, but Meg resisted the urge to trust her. "What does he know about my life? What do you? You are strangers to me!"

"He sees people, Meg. He is always watching."

Meg dropped into the chair. She found her neck would no longer support her heavy head and allowed it to fall onto her hands. The first tears fell with the gentle hand on her back. "Let it go," Molly whispered, "you don't need to carry it here."

The wall she had constructed to protect herself from her guilt collapsed in the cozy kitchen with the kind young woman. She sobbed as she hadn't since her fall from grace, her breaths coming in deep, ragged gulps. Molly's youthful appearance disguised the understanding of an old soul who knew how to be still and let Meg cry out her grief.

The kitchen grew brighter as Bobby pushed like a ball of energy through the door, dragging Nick behind him. With the blissful ignorance of the very young, Bobby demanded his mother's attention, completely unaware of the weeping woman she was comforting. "Mama, did you finish those cookies? Can I have one, please? One of the chocolate ones with the red frosting? Nick wants one, too, don't you, Nick?"

"Chocolate with red frosting is my favorite, Bobby," Nick said smiling, but he was focused on Meg's tear-stained face. He held her eyes and would not let her look away.

"How about some tea with that cookie, Nick?" Molly asked.

"Thank you, Molly." When Nick sat down at the table, Molly put the cookie in front of him and poured his tea. She collected her son and said, "Com'on, Bobby. Let's go eat your cookie while we listen to your sister practice her piano."

Nick waited patiently while Meg took a deep breath, wiped her eyes and blew her nose with her napkin. When he felt she was ready, he asked without pretense, "What is it that you think you have done?"

"Don't you know? You seem to know everything else about me."

"I want to hear you say it."

She broke free of his gaze, swallowed hard and struggled with her pain and guilt. "I can't," she said finally. "You'll hate me." And why shouldn't he? She hated herself.

Nick sat calmly with his hands folded on the table, watching her closely but saying nothing. Muffled strains of a novice piano player floated on the air but would not distract Megan. She found the first hints of forgiveness in his patience, but she still could not lay out her crimes for him to see.

She barely perceived that Nick stood until he pulled her up into his strong arms. She could hear his heart and feel its steady, rhythmic beat. As he tightened his embrace, she felt for the first time that there was a safe place in the world where she could escape the horrors of her life. He held her without a word until Bobby burst into the kitchen, looking for another cookie, completely oblivious to the private moment he had interrupted.

It was not lost on his mother, however, who checked their faces and smiled with approval. She leaned in to speak to Meg in confidence. "Better? I can see that you are. He's a miracle, this man, isn't he?"

Nick reached for Meg's hand. "Come on," he said smoothly, "walk with me."

Molly handed Meg a coat which she took automatically. When they stepped outside she pulled the coat tight against the frigid air. Curiosity overwhelmed all of her other thoughts as she took in her surroundings. "Where are we? We must have travelled a long way from where we were. It's too cold for England in October."

"Yes," he confirmed.

"Where are we?" she asked again.

"We have come far to the north, as you guessed."

"No," she demanded stubbornly. "Where exactly have we come to and how did we get here so fast?"

"I've told you, we've come to the north, to my home, and you know that we came here through the fogou."

"Come on," she said, frustrated. "I need to know more than that."

"That's enough for now." His voice was kind but firm.

She wasn't going to let it go. "Ok, then. What about you? Who are you? Why are we here?" She noticed she was sounding a little shrill.

"Peace, Megan." That was it, the end of the conversation.

He led her into different shops, where the happy proprietors proudly showed their wares. In one window a taffy puller worked a six foot log of pink taffy, folding it in and over and back on itself until it would be soft enough to eat. In another window a man worked two similarly-sized portions of hot sugar into one long stick of red and white for candy canes. Inside they found chocolate truffles painted with colorful syrups that were works of art, too beautiful to eat. Eat they did, however, when the young man behind the counter eagerly offered them samples, treating Nick like a great celebrity. Nick praised the artistry of the strawberry-shaped truffle so that the candy maker stood straighter and taller from his attention, then took a bite and closed his eyes as though it took him to the pinnacle of pleasure. The creamy chocolate melted in Meg's mouth, unlike any other candy she had ever tasted, driving out all thoughts but the ecstasy of the experience. This was no ordinary chocolate.

The next shop housed an enormous loom. The woman stopped her work when they entered and proudly displayed her hand-made sweaters, scarves, and blankets. The yarn she worked with was the deep, infinite turquoise of a clear, fall day. Nick lifted the skein and stroked Meg's face with it. She had never felt anything softer. He gifted the weaver with one of his dazzling smiles, calling her work "remarkable" and "unmatched by any other he had ever seen." His attention caused her to flush bright red and sway slightly on her feet. Meg realized the woman had made the sweater she wore and marveled aloud at its plum color, nuanced with shades of dark and light like the actual, living fruit. Instantly she had a friend.

They entered the next shop at precisely four o'clock to the chiming of dozens of clocks of various sizes and shapes. The deepest, reverberating gong came from a grandfather with a shiny, brass pendulum as large as a dinner plate and a woodland scene carved into the top above the golden clock face. The sweetest tinkling chimes came from the mantle clock with a face hand-painted with pink Victorian roses and lilies-of-the-valley. One cuckoo sounded a few minutes late,

31

nodding frantically to catch up with its shop-mates. The owner reset its time as though petting a favorite dog. He led them to his workbench and demonstrated the mechanism he was perfecting for his newest clock. Instead of a cuckoo, a conductor appeared at the top and tapped the hour with his baton. Ballerinas in floral tutus came out through the little doors, whirling to the Nutcracker's "Waltz of the Flowers". Nick grinned and congratulated the clockmaker with an enthusiastic slap on the back. Meg was enchanted.

Though there were other shops to see, she was ready for a break when Nick pulled her off the path into the countryside. The sun set in an explosion of pinks and oranges and purples, casting a rosy glow on everything around them. Clouds rolled in and lit up like fireworks in the bright waning light.

Nick led her to sit on an old stone wall, stretching his long legs comfortably in spite of the cold, hard perch.

"Thank you for this remarkable tour," she said, "but I still don't understand why you brought me here."

"It was time for you to stop running."

"So you whisked me away to a place where I have no idea where I am?" she asked skeptically.

"You will go back when you are ready."

Trapped in his intense gaze, she realized that fighting him would be useless, but she couldn't imagine that she would ever be ready to go back. "What if I don't want to go back?" she said.

He put his arm around her shoulders and pulled her closer. Tucked into his body, warm and comfortable in spite of the stone wall, she wondered why she would ever want to leave.

Chapter 5

In the days that followed Meg discovered that being busy was the best antidote for a heartsick soul. She found that she had a talent for candy making and loved being instructed in the vanishing art of creating sugarplums and Turkish delight by the chief candy maker. Though not so skilled at the loom, she spent time attending the weaver, doing chores around the shop and learning the secrets of her remarkable dyes and soft fabrics. She stepped into the toymaker's shop to discover a small group of boys lining up wooden soldiers in red and blue on opposing battle lines. Little girls sat nearby on a rug, cradling dolls of varying skin, hair and eye colors. A large wicker basket on the floor held a collection of painted wooden tops unlike any she had seen since she was a child. With a glance over her shoulder to be sure no one was watching, she pulled the string and sent one spinning across the floor. When she went to retrieve it, she found herself facing a colorful display of nutcrackers dressed as everything from traditional soldiers to shoemakers to football players.

Attached to the clockmaker's shop was another one selling all kinds of musical boxes. Far from being irritated by her intrusions, the music box maker relished her enthusiasm for his creations, allowing her to play as many and as often as she liked. He stood taller and grinned at her. She so cherished their melodies that she played them one at a time, allowing each to roll to its end before starting the next. Her favorite, a large lacquered box with a beautiful inlaid rose, had an old fashioned crank on the side. When she opened the top it played "Lo How a Rose 'ere Blooming".

She found herself drawn to the children, following them in makeshift parades through town or hunting treasures in the thick fallen leaves and needles of the nearby forest. Everything became a plaything to them, stick or stone or feather, and the world opened to her in a whole new way. She had forgotten how much she enjoyed playing with her nephews and thought of how quickly they would grow beyond the age of innocence and wonder while she was gone from their lives.

Molly's tavern was home. In the evenings the dining room filled with the residents of the town, who adopted her easily as one of their own. Nick came there every night, smiling and friendly, reminding Meg of a beloved king who moved among his people with great affection, although he wasn't quite one of them. The same deference did not apply to the children who danced around him, singing and climbing into his lap to whisper secrets in his ear. The place next to him was respectfully left vacant for her, and she occupied it gladly whenever she wasn't helping Molly. Molly told her that Nick had often brought outsiders to their town, but his appearances in the tavern had never been as regular as they had since she arrived, and he had never, ever reserved a place for anyone at his side.

Every day Nick materialized mid-afternoon, took her hand and led her on a rambling trek through forest and field. He was quiet for the most part, giving no details of his background, not his age or his birthplace or his family, but in their companionable silence she felt she came to know him better than anyone else she had ever known in her life. He showed her the wonders of the world around them like a proud father, eager that she not miss any miracle of winter berry or flower. They laughed together at the escapades of fussy squirrels and argumentative birds and watched a dozen sunsets from their perch on the stone wall.

One night as the revelers were leaving the tavern, she and Nick could see through the doors and windows that the night was almost as light as day. The clouds of the afternoon had dropped their snow and moved on, leaving the town and countryside blanketed in a beautiful coverlet of icy white. The full, silver moon outshone its nearest stars in the cold, crisp air. The adults moved off with laughter and back-slapping while the children ran, jumped and slid, falling down to make snow angels, and scooping up balls of snow to hurl at each other and their parents.

Nick and Meg left the crowd and strolled away from the lights of the town. The snow muffled every sound except for the crunch of their footsteps breaking its pristine surface. Gentle breezes had blown it into frozen waves, each of which reflected the moonlight like dozens of diamonds sparkling across a gently pulsing sea.

Although he was always frugal with his words, it was nonetheless unusual for them to walk so long in complete silence. "What is it?" she asked, afraid of the answer, but knowing in her heart what it would be.

"It is time for you to leave."

Like a petulant child, she refused to take another step. "I won't go."

In the bright moonlight she could see his face clearly. His jaw was set, his eyes unyielding. "I am pleased for you to say so, but you must."

"Why?"

"I brought you here to grow strong again, and so you are. Now you must go back into the world and do the things on your list."

"List? What list?"

"We are all assigned tasks," he replied. "It is time for you to be about yours."

"Tasks?" she asked.

He stopped and tipped up her chin to look directly into her eyes. Stroking the hair from her face, he leaned in.

It felt like a first kiss. Not just their first kiss, but the first time he had ever kissed anyone, tentative and tender. He kissed her again, wrapping her in his arms and pulling her tight against him. Her thoughts split into the thousand diamond sparkles of the snow shine. When their breath was heavy and hanging as a mist in the cold air, they split apart, but he allowed only millimeters of the frigid night to come between them. She waited for him to speak, but as usual he said nothing.

She broke the silence, "You don't want me to leave."

"No."

"But you tell me I must."

"Yes."

"It must be important, what I have to do."

"Yes."

"Tell me."

"Not now. Tomorrow will be soon enough to say."

She shuddered and could not say if it was because of the cold or her dismay at leaving him.

"Don't worry," he smiled. "I'm not going to make you stay out here in the cold. My house is not far."

He led her up a hill they not explored before. As they crested the top she saw that they had circled around to where his house, nestled in a secluded terrace, had a perfect view of the sleeping village below.

What would a place where such a man lived look like? It was not at all what she expected. Like its owner, the old, red Victorian could only be described by it contradictions. Large and impressive, at the same time it was friendly and inviting. The large front porch with its rocking chairs had a perfect view of the village below, and yet she wondered who sat in the chairs when their owner was so solitary and mysterious. Every tall, shutterless window glowed warmly as though full of life and family, yet she was almost certain he had none.

The fragrant fir wreaths on the doors were harbingers of the wonderful scents within, a mixture of fir, cinnamon and cloves. The interior reminded her of a museum, but not a stuffy, don't-dare-touch marble hall. It seemed more like the collection of a person who running out of room for his memories. Casually framed artwork of dozens of children lined the foyer walls. Though a few reflected the early buds of real talent, most childishly depicted Nick, or zoo animals, or their families, or Santa Claus, or Christmas trees, but some were the indefinable creations of unbridled imaginations. Toys, music boxes, and *objets d'art* covered every horizontal surface and reflected every style from innocent childhood to magnificent Renaissance.

Nick led her into a library with book shelves floor-to-ceiling on every wall. Books crowded each other on the shelves and loose volumes lay around the room on an assortment of ornate tables and overstuffed chairs. She checked a few and the variety astonished her: a dog-eared *Odyssey* in Greek, *Beowulf* in Old English,

Les Miserables in French, a first edition of Twain's *Huckleberry Finn*, a tea stained copy of *Winnie the Pooh*. One shelf had multiple editions of *A Christmas Carol* by Dickens, while another boasted a collection of children's illustrated versions of "A Visit from St. Nicholas" by Clement Moore.

"You like to read," she observed.

"Yes," he replied, looking at his collection fondly.

"I like to read, too."

"I know."

"Your tastes are very eclectic."

"Great ideas can occur in unexpected places."

She sat where he indicated on a comfortable loveseat facing a brightly burning fire. An enormous fir tree sparkling with hundreds of twinkling white lights stood proudly in one corner.

"Does someone else live here with you?"

"No."

"But the fire was already burning when we got here. Surely you didn't set it to burn all day? And the house is all lit up. Do you leave every light on all the time?"

"Meg, aren't there more important questions you'd like to ask?"

Her Southern upbringing made her sensitive to his subtext. "Yes, but I don't expect I'll get any answers."

"Try."

Her arsenal of questions was at the ready. "What is this place? Where is it? Have you always lived here?"

"Like you, I was looking for purpose and peace. I found it here."

"How did you find it?"

"I explored the fogou that you know and discovered that it led to this place of serenity and beauty. Once I experienced it I couldn't bring myself to leave."

"And yet you make others leave."

"Only for a while," he said affectionately. "When you have accomplished your tasks, you may return, if you wish. Many others before you have."

"Is that how everyone else came to be here?"

"Some."

"When did you come?"

"A long, long time ago. I am older than I look."

"How much older?"

He smiled. "Let's just say 'I'm as old as my tongue and a little bit older than my teeth'."

"*Miracle on 34th Street*," she said, recalling a movie she had seen numerous times. An unusual comment from a person who looked barely over thirty.

"Jonathan Swift," he corrected. "Anything else?"

"Lots," she replied, "for example, have you ever been married?"

"No."

"Ever come close?"

"No," He moved his attention to the crackling fire. "I never considered it before now."

She fell back against the pillows. Did he mean what she thought he meant? Did she dare hope? She could not see his face, could not read the emotion behind his words. "But you said that you have brought others here."

"I have brought others to our village, and they have gone back into the world. Some of them returned, and I call them friends. But you are not like they were."

"What do you mean?" The precious hope of her hopeless soul could not be trusted to misunderstanding.

"I find I am more invested in you than I have been in any of the others."

"Invested?"

The words came hard to this man characteristically so sparse with them. "I find myself seeking your company."

Emotions played across his face like sunlight and shadow through leaves dancing in the breeze. Affection. Pain. Desire. Despair. Resolve.

"Don't send me away," she begged.

"I have no choice. You have no choice. It is what we must do." He drew himself straight. "It is why we are here."

"Then let me go and do what I must so I can come back." She steeled her resolve to match his.

He stood up and held out his hand without comment. He led her silently through the snow, down the quiet main street to the tavern. In the dark a single candle glowed in the window. Nick pulled her close for one final kiss and strode off into the darkness.

Chapter 6

Nick arrived early the next morning as Meg, Molly and the children were finishing breakfast. Molly served Nick and Meg steaming cups of tea at the kitchen table before she herded her family out to give them privacy.

"You have a gift," he began, indicating the piece of parchment he held as calmly as though he was giving her directions to the grocery store.

"Me?" One sentence in, and he was already wrong. It had all been a mistake. She should've known. "I don't think so."

"You see through to the truth of people, although you seem to be blind when it comes to yourself."

She screwed her face into scornful disbelief but swallowed the retorts that bubbled up.

He pressed on. "You have wondered what we do here. We are in the business of helping people."

"The *business* of helping people? How's that?"

She wondered why she hadn't noticed before that the worry lines in his brow never fully disappeared, and there were permanently etched laugh lines at the corners of his eyes that crinkled when he smiled. He had said that he was older than he looked. "Everything we make, everything we do," he began, "exists solely for the purpose of relieving the burdens of those who are suffering. We look for those who hide their need behind joyous living and service to others. There is plenty of help to be had for those who ask, but some in the most desperate situations soldier on without

41

complaint to the point of absolute devastation. We want to save them from that."

"How? And how do you know who they are?"

"We get messages from those who see their need."

"What messages? Who sends the messages? How do they find you?"

"They come to us like the falling rain, hundreds of them. Unfortunately, we cannot help them all."

"What do you do?"

"Whatever we can as our resources allow."

"Resources?"

"Have you seen money change hands since you have been here? Our people work every day, but have you seen any surplus of their products?"

"No," she replied, replaying her time in the village like a video in her mind's eye.

"Some of their needs can be satisfied by the things we make here. We simply drop them on their doorsteps."

She thought of the shopkeeper's comments that now seemed so long ago. "Folks need clothes, they appear. Folks need food, it appears. Folks need money, it appears. No muss, no fuss, no by-your-leave."

"What if they need money?" she asked.

"You would be surprised how often a need for money can be solved with a different kind of gift. However, we have shops all over the world where we sell our goods and put the money in the treasury," he answered patiently. "It can be distributed as the need arises."

"So these few people provide for the needs of hundreds?"

"There are fogous and souterrains all over the world that all lead to different parts of this country, and there are other villages to handle their needs."

"And you are in charge of them all?"

"I am. But this one is my home."

"All this is very nice," she replied, maintaining her skepticism, "but where do I fit in?"

"As I said, you see the truth of things. The messages we get come from sources that are pretty reliable for letting us know that a problem exists, but not very good at determining exactly what the trouble is or the best solution. We want you to go into the situation, meet the people, and determine where the real problem lies."

"Whatever about my life makes you think I am qualified to do this?" How could he look at her like that? With such kindness and affection?

"Your qualifications are so obvious that only you cannot see them."

"I don't share your confidence," she replied, despondent.

He gently lifted her chin so she faced him. "I have enough confidence for both of us."

"Fine," she said, still doubtful but unable to say no to his unwavering conviction, "so what do I do?"

"We will see that you get to where you need to be and have the means to find the person you've been sent to know."

"You know, this seems a little Big Brother. Who are you to decide who needs what and who deserves what? And watching people who don't know they're being watched is a little creepy, don't you think?"

"In the past, we were generous without qualification, but the need has outgrown our ability to help. When we realized that there were many other groups delivering aid and many people asking for things they do not need, we rethought our mission. That is when we decided we could best serve those who do not ask for help. It is more challenging but ultimately more satisfying."

"You will help me do this?"

"Yes."

"Okay." She resigned herself to his insistence. "Let's get started."

All of her suspicions melted at the expression on his face. His gaze was so tender that it made her dizzy. "The first name on your list is Lyda Andrews. She lives in the Smoky Mountains near Gatlinburg, Tennessee."

Chapter 7

Lyda

Nick gave her no chance for long goodbyes. He lifted her onto the back of the big white horse called Snow and rode with her through another long, dark, seemingly endless tunnel which put them out in a well-hidden cave entrance in the forests of the Appalachian Mountains. How they managed to cross the Atlantic Ocean in space and time Meg could not say, but given all the wondrous mysteries she had seen and heard, she decided not to press him for details. Leaving Snow concealed in the cave with a bucket of oats, they hiked out of the woods to a picnic site parking lot where they found an unlocked car with the keys under the driver's seat. An accordion file rested on the passenger seat. In the first section Meg found an exquisitely drawn postcard. *Lyda Andrews* it said in flowing script. On the back in the same flowing script was an address in Gatlinburg, Tennessee and one cryptic comment. *She often paints at the scenic overlooks*. She turned to Nick for explanation, but he was nowhere to be seen. He had disappeared.

She sucked air into her lungs' full capacity and blew it out slowly.

She quickly discovered the reason for the name Smoky Mountains. The clouds sat so low she could barely see to the other side of the road where the scenic stops overlooked the currently invisible mountains and valleys. The road was steep and relatively narrow. Grateful to be on the side away from the treacherous edge, she found spotting Lyda's artist's venue a nearly impossible task. Honking traffic was backing up behind her as she looked for some sign that she had found the right place.

Suddenly the sun cut through the fog and revealed a magnificent panorama of the evergreen mountains and a fair, level place from which to view it. She pulled over and let the others go by. Some waved thanks. Others honked in anger, and one belligerent teenager gave her the finger. When she got out of the car to walk off the stress, she found the artist at her easel, off the path where Meg would never have seen her if she hadn't stopped. She made a mental note to ask Nick if he also controlled the weather.

Meg stood back for a while, watching the older woman create pure beauty on a blank canvas. She had expected an impressive landscape of the magnificent mountains, but instead Lyda carefully crafted one exquisite golden yellow maple leaf, a straggler hanging on long after all the others had fallen in the Tennessee autumn. She captured every vein and freckle, every nuance of color and play of light, all in vivid definition against the misty blue-gray-green background of the nearby hills.

She looked around for the artist's model and saw it hanging, small and insignificant above their heads. "Boy," she said aloud, "I would never even have seen that leaf if I hadn't seen it on your canvas."

The woman smiled without looking up. "I see the mountains every day. I have painted their splendor dozens of times. Now when I come out to paint I look for the things I missed when my vision was too broad."

"You are very good."

"Thank you, dear."

"Do you sell your paintings?"

46

"Why do you ask?"

"You're so good, and I think I would like to see your other paintings and maybe buy one to keep."

"Oh, every now and then I will put a few in the artists' cooperative, but mostly, no, I only paint for myself."

"My name is Megan. Do you mind if I watch for a while?" Meg asked, sitting on the ground at the artist's feet like a kindergartner on the classroom rug.

"Lyda Andrews," she replied looking down at her audience. "You want to watch me paint? I can hardly imagine anything less interesting."

"It's interesting to me."

"Why? Are you an artist?"

Meg shook her head. "Nope, I can't even color inside the lines. That's why the process is so fascinating."

"You are certainly welcome to sit here for as long as you please."

They sat in silence as small, scattered groups of people stopped, looked and left. At the end of the hour Lyda stood up to stretch. She had trouble straightening up, bracing her back with her hands and pushing her spine into place. She shifted her weight from one leg to the other until she felt stable enough to take a step. When she did, she almost stepped on Meg.

"Good gracious, girl, I forgot you were there. How have you been sitting on that cold, hard ground all this time?"

Meg pushed herself up and found that she, too, was stiff from sitting too long. She did a few stretches to loosen up while she spoke to Lyda. "I was enjoying watching you so much that I forgot where I was."

The older woman looked doubtful. "You're pulling my leg."

"No, really. I was trying to see the leaf the way you did. Your attention to detail is mesmerizing. Even though we were looking at the same thing, you saw something completely different than I did."

Lyda looked suspicious, certain that she was being played by a young person who couldn't possibly think an old mountain artist was so interesting. "It's just a leaf."

"Not in your eyes."

"Well, if you are being honest, then I am glad you enjoyed it."

"Thank you. Will you be painting again tomorrow?"

"Not here. I have finished this one."

"May I come to watch where you are going next?"

"Are you serious?" When Meg nodded with as much sincerity as she could put into a nod, Lyda said, "I've picked a point near the river for my next painting. If you really want to watch, I'll be outside of town, near the ranger's station."

Back in her car, Meg found a GPS had been mounted on the windshield and a hotel room card key left in the next section of the accordion file. She looked around, hoping to catch Nick nearby, but she sat alone in the growing darkness. Anxiety replaced anticipation as she contemplated navigating the unfamiliar winding roads in the dark, a steep drop-off into oblivion waiting at the end of a wrong turn. Searching for a map, she lifted the accordion file off the passenger seat. Then she realized the glowing screen of the GPS detailed her route. Thanks to the GPS she found her way without incident to the Brookside Hotel, the name on the room key.

Meg enjoyed her night in Gatlinburg, even though every restaurant and shop was a tourist trap. She bought fudge and took it into the *Believe It or Not* freak show. She cracked the window in her room and bundled up against the cold air. The thundering roar of the mountain river eased her anxieties and gave her a deep, restful sleep.

The next morning, after the GPS proved unreliable since she didn't have the address of the ranger' station, she had to get directions from one restaurant and two gas stations. Meg finally found the ranger's station. She recognized the only other car in the parking lot as the one Lyda had left in the day before.

Looking across the meadow, she saw Lyda in the distance sitting on her stool, a fresh, blank canvas on her easel. Megan moved quickly across the open space, genuinely excited to see what treasure the artist had discovered for the day.

"You made it," Lyda said as she walked up. "I didn't know if you would really come, but I brought you a chair, just in case. No need for you to sit on that hard ground while you watch me paint."

"Thank you so much." Touched by her kindness, Meg smiled. "What have you discovered today?"

"Would you like to guess?" the older woman teased.

"From a blank canvas? I have no idea."

"You wanted to watch me paint, so watch. Tell me when you think you have worked it out."

She laid the background with the blacks, grays, browns and dark greens of the forest floor. More like a sculptor molding clay than a painter, she began to craft a riverbank from the rocks, dirt and moss by playing with shadow and light. As she filled in the details a craggy root began to appear and attach itself to the long lines of a shadowy tree.

Meg looked at the opposite side of the river to see what Lyda saw. It was as she had drawn, a tree clinging to life with it roots naked to the frigid, rushing water. "It's that tree," Meg said triumphantly, "the one over there with its roots exposed."

"Very good," Lyda responded, pleased.

A natural teacher, Lyda began to talk as she painted. "Do you understand what a wonder it is for that tree to survive? It's a common ash, a tree like any of thousands of others that grow in these mountains. But that one is special. It has stepped outside its ordinariness and survived in unsurvivable conditions. Have you ever overwatered a plant and watched it die? This tree is the same kind as many others that are farther off the riverbank whose roots get just the right amount of water to keep them healthy. But this one survives where the water runs over its roots every day, all the time, without giving the tree a chance to dry out or catch its breath. During the spring thaw the river stampedes like wild horses rushing down from the mountains and floods everything on its banks, so that the roots sit completely submerged for days on end. This time of year the water that touches it is so cold that it would be ice if it were not moving. Still the tree survives. It thrives. When I come back in the spring it will be covered with dainty green buds that give no indication how resilient it is, how much tougher than all the others of its kind standing so close by."

The lesson stopped and the teacher fell silent. Her hands dropped into her lap and her chin fell to her chest.

"What's wrong?" Meg asked.

"Nothing, dear," she replied quietly, brushing away a tear.

"Com'on. What's up?"

"I won't be here to see the buds in the spring."

"Why?"

"My children are moving me to Ohio to be closer to them so they can take care of me when I get feeble."

"Whew!" Meg exclaimed, "I thought you were dying."

"No, dear. Just a little death of the soul."

"What do you mean?"

"To say these mountains are my home is like saying my painting is a hobby. They are my heart, my soul, the very air that I breathe. I feel the seasons change, and live my life based on their cycle. I have learned to be so still that raccoons and foxes will come within inches of where I am sitting. I can close my eyes and know the different birds by their songs. I can tell you when every bush will flower in the spring, and every tree will drop its leaves in the fall. I am not merely happy here. I am as much a part of its landscape as the tree, the leaf, or the river."

"Have you talked to your children about your feelings?"

"They know. They have apologized and apologized, and I don't want them to feel guilty about doing what they think is best. They love me, and they are worried about me out here by myself. They need me close if something happens, and they would rather move me now, while we have control of the situation, rather than later when it is an emergency."

"Lyda, I'm so sorry."

Lyda pulled herself together. "Oh dear, don't be sorry. Do you know how lucky I am that my children love me? That they want to take care of me? And I've been with these mountains far longer than most people. I'll be taking them with me wherever I go."

"And you have your paintings."

"And I have my paintings."

"I would like very much to see more of them."

"What are your plans for Thanksgiving?"

She was caught off guard. "I'm sorry, what? Thanksgiving?"

"Thanksgiving. Tomorrow. Are there people expecting you for dinner?"

Meg shook her head slowly, stupefied by the passage of time. "No. To be honest, I had forgotten all about the holiday."

Lyda smiled. "I thought so. Why don't you come and eat with me? I'm alone as well, and you will give me a reason to cook. I was an excellent cook in my day, but there's hardly a reason to prepare a great meal when it's just for me."

Meg couldn't believe the words that came out of her own mouth. "I'd love to." Love to? This woman was a stranger to her, and she was going to her house for dinner?

"Excellent." She seemed genuinely excited. "It's a date." She wrote her address on a scrap of paper she pulled out of her pocket, and then she sent Meg on her way with a hug and a pat on the back.

Meg arrived for dinner the next day, requisite hostess wine in hand. The road to Lyda's house was a gated dirt path that materialized from a secluded corner of the ranger station parking lot. Meg left her car and hiked into the shadows of the forest, wondering if the woodlands belonged to Lyda or were part of the park. Snow had begun to fall and pile up against the roots of the trees, and she enjoyed its beauty as she walked until her old friend anxiety raised its choke hold on her throat and pulled her backwards as she fought against it to move forward. Her job was to play intelligence agent with this woman, and here was an opportunity she could hardly ignore.

Smoke rose like an invitation from the chimney of the cozy log cottage, and brightly lit windows beckoned her in and eased her fears. She crossed the porch, its railings already decked with Christmas garlands, and knocked on the heavy front door. The vision that greeted her was straight out of sixties television, dressed for dinner in a tailored skirt and blouse with a classic string of pearls. "Welcome, welcome," she said sincerely. "I'm so pleased that you're here."

The entire length of the house was taken by one large room with the fireplace in the middle and the kitchen at one end. Lyda had already decorated her Christmas tree, wringing every moment she could out of her last holiday in the mountains. An astonishing collection of paintings left little of the walls visible. Though most were in Lyda's distinctive style, Meg noticed that several were done by other artists. The picture of the leaf that she had been working on at the scenic overlook sat on one easel, and the half-finished river root sat on another. Lyda noticed when Meg looked closely at the family pictures on the mantle. "My children and their children," she said affectionately. "That one of all of us together was taken when they came to visit last summer. The children loved playing on the rocks in the river," she trailed off sadly.

Meg sought to lighten the mood. "Any of them artists like you?"

Lyda brightened. "My granddaughter. The little one there. Her name is Clara. I have a few of her masterpieces in here with all the others."

Meg noticed the childish drawings here and there among the glorious landscapes and near photography quality still lifes. Though obviously the work of young hands, the perceptive vision and gift for putting it on paper shone through. "Her grandmother's granddaughter," she commented.

"I believe time will show that her talent far exceeds mine," Lyda replied proudly. "I didn't have nearly so good an eye at her age." She paused to admire the closest Clara original of the giant rocks in the rushing river. "Come now and sit down," she invited. "Dinner is ready."

Meg moved to the table sparkling with fine china and crystal. "Wow," she exclaimed on an expelled breath, "this is beautiful. I am so honored that you would go to all this trouble for me." The feast on the table was enough for a family of eight. "My goodness, Lyda, all this food for us? You have totally outdone yourself."

Lyda smiled. "I got a little carried away," she said modestly, "but I really do love to cook, and I so seldom have a reason. Besides, there are certain dishes one must have for Thanksgiving, whether for a group of two or twenty."

Indeed, the menu was traditional Thanksgiving, but the food was better than any she had eaten since the last time she ate at her mother's table. The turkey tasted moister than it had a right to, and the gravy was perfectly seasoned, tasting of rosemary and ground pepper instead of sautéed flour. Every dish tasted like a culinary masterpiece, from the dressing with chopped pecans and cranberries to the devilishly buttered mashed potatoes to the creamy sweet potatoes with marshmallows, straight out of a church fundraising cookbook. The homemade yeast rolls begged her to eat every one, and the classic pumpkin pie with a twist, whipped into a mousse-like confection, melted in her mouth. Every dish became an immediate addiction, and Meg couldn't stop eating until she had to lean back and unbutton the waist of her pants.

"Lyda, I don't believe I have ever eaten so well," Meg said enthusiastically. "You are going to have to roll me back to the hotel. I'm so full I can't move at all."

Lyda laughed. "Then I have accomplished my goal. Come sit by the fire and have coffee."

Meg cradled the warm mug in her hands and sat sideways on the sofa to face her hostess. "I hope I'm not out of line for asking, but I can't help but notice there is no husband in the family pictures."

"Not out of line at all," Lyda replied, "we are long divorced."

"I didn't mean to open an old wound."

"It is scarred over well beyond being opened again," Lyda remarked, shifting her gaze to the fire. "He was not a good man, not a good husband or father. In fact, he was rather a beast. I stayed with him far longer than I should have, but back in those days one didn't air one's dirty little secrets in public."

"Did he hit you?"

"No. No bruises. Not for me or the children. But he had a ferocious temper and made our lives quite hellish. We never knew who would walk through the door at the end of the day, the monster or the man."

"I'm so sorry."

Lyda smiled and placed a comforting hand on Meg's hand. "Don't be. It happened a long time ago, and I have long since made my peace with it. The mountains," she said indicating the gallery of art around them, "the mountains have healed me. They can heal you, too."

"What?" Meg asked, alarmed. "What makes you think I need healing?"

"Why else would you be spending Thanksgiving alone with a stranger?"

"Funny, I'd forgotten you were a stranger."

"What a wonderful compliment."

"It's true."

"This has been a splendid Thanksgiving, Megan. This year I am most thankful for you."

Meg was touched into silence. How could there be a person left in the world as sweet and kind as the woman before her? She turned her attention to the paintings that captured the mountains in every season, from every possible point of view. Sitting here in the wood cabin, surrounded by a forest verdant even in the cold winter months, Meg wondered how this woman could live separated from the place so intricately a part of who she was. She wanted to say she was sorry. Sorry that Lyda had to leave her home. Sorry that the world was not a kinder place so that older people could choose where to live out the balance of their days, where families lived close always and no one had to move away from the place she loved. She wanted to fix it and make everything work out as it should. But how? What could she do? Would Nick come in now and make things right? Though her heart swelled, Meg kept her thoughts to herself so as not to upset the happy mood of their evening.

It was, however, getting late. "Let's do these dishes," she said with a smile, "I need to get back before I turn into a pumpkin, and you make me into one of your wonderful pies."

Lyda laughed. "You are my guest and you will most definitely not do any dishes. Not in my house. I have plenty of time to take care of them tomorrow."

"Let me at least help you put the food away."

"And let you see me taking salacious little nibbles here and there? Absolutely not." She actually grinned, eyes sparkling in her elegantly perfect face. "Shall I walk you back to your car? It's a long way in the dark alone."

"And then you have to walk back by yourself? No, I think I can handle it."

Lyda took the painting of the leaf off the easel and presented it to Meg. "Please accept this, Meg, in memory of our brief but happy friendship."

Stunned, Meg could barely read the message on the painting. At the bottom she had inscribed *Beauty lives everywhere, my precious friend. All my love, Lyda.* "I don't know what to say," she stammered. "It is a treasure beyond words."

"Not really," Lyda replied. "But I am glad you are pleased."

Meg squeezed Lyda in an embrace tight enough to make up for all the ones they would never have.

"Farewell, Megan."

"And you. Thank you so much for a memorable evening."

Lyda watched from the doorway until Meg passed out of sight.

As she walked along with a flashlight lighting the bare dirt ahead of her, Meg's contented mood was accosted by the awareness of the dark woods and the eerie silence. She felt exposed, as though dangerous, unfriendly eyes could be watching from places she could not see. She quickened her pace anxiously, trying to walk fast without tripping on the uneven ground.

Then she heard them. Were those footsteps on the path behind her? She kept moving, but held her breath to block out the sounds of her living body. She might have stilled the sounds, but she could not stop the painful *bum, bum, bum* of her heart against the inside of her chest. Not only were there steps, but she could also hear cool, steady breathing. Afraid to turn her flashlight to illuminate her pursuer, she tried to rush on without running, hoping to get someplace safe before he caught up with her. An exposed tree root caught her foot on a poorly placed step, and she felt herself going down. As she reached out to brace for impact with the rock-hard ground, she found herself steadied by her ever-watching savior.

Nick.

"How do you do that?" she panted, willing her heart to slow.

"Do what?" he asked, his face unreadable in the darkness.

"Just appear without any warning at all."

"Maybe you're not paying close enough attention."

She wished he could see her perturbed expression. But then again, maybe among his many other miraculous talents he could see in the dark like a cat. She felt the rumble of his chuckle against her cheek, and thought she must have hit close to the mark.

"So," he said, "tell me about Lyda."

"She is amazing," Megan began enthusiastically. "You probably can't tell in the dark, but this painting is a miracle. She sees things that other people never would and puts them on the canvas so vividly that they are better than photographs."

"Did you enjoy watching her paint?"

"I really did. It was like watching the craftsmen in your village. No detail is left untended, and yet she relishes every second of it with no impatience for the tedious nature of her task."

"That is a marvel," Nick agreed. "So in what way does she need our help?"

Megan sighed. "Her children are moving her away from here to live with them in Ohio. She is devastated, and they are so selfish. Just because their lives are busy, they use that as an excuse to not find a way for her to stay."

"Did she say they were selfish?"

"No. She said she understands and appreciates them. That is the kind of woman she is, Nick, wonderful, kind and understanding. She doesn't deserve what they are doing to her."

"Perhaps she's right to understand them. Maybe they are doing the right thing."

Megan was taken back. Were they here to help Lyda or not? "What do you mean? Aren't we supposed to take care of her problem? Aren't we supposed to see that she gets what she deserves?"

"Megan, what if being cared for by her children is what she deserves?"

Frustrated, she exclaimed, "Then why am I here? If you're just going to let this happen to her, why do you need me to tell you it is unfair?"

"I don't need for you to judge the rightness of what is happening, Meg," he replied evenly. "I need for you to tell me what her problem is and if it is something that we can help."

"Absolutely. She survived a miserable marriage, raised her children to live successful, happy lives in spite of it and still finds joy in life. She is kind and loving enough to take in a complete stranger for a Thanksgiving feast, and not just with a quick easy meal. She went all out, making spectacular food and setting a beautiful, elegant table. Nothing was done halfway."

"Like her paintings. No detail left untended."

"Exactly."

"What else?"

"She shares her love of art with everyone she meets. Her walls are covered with the work of her students, as well as her own. The world is a much better, more beautiful place because she is in it."

"That's what I was looking for," Nick replied.

"So if you're not going to make it so she can stay here, what are you going to do?"

She should have expected his evasive answer. "We'll take care of it."

"Take care of what? How?"

They arrived at the parking lot, and Nick rode with her back to her hotel. He accompanied her to her room, but made no romantic advances like she hoped he would. She fell asleep with him sitting at the desk making notes on the Brookside Hotel stationery.

Chapter 8

Ophelia

In the morning he was gone, and she wondered briefly if she had merely dreamed his visit. She knew it had been real when she found that he had left another accordion folder on the desk. The card in the front pocket said *Ophelia Flores* in the same beautiful script as before and on the back there was an address in Brooklyn, New York.

It was a long drive, but a familiar one. Meg didn't need the GPS to know that once she got on I-95 it was a straight shot to New York, although she usually took the Metroliner from DC when she went up for the weekend. Navigating Brooklyn proved a little trickier, and she couldn't imagine having to do it without the GPS.

The back of the card had a picture of Ophelia and listed her place of work. Megan sat in the car staring at the Beach View Nursing Home and Rehabilitation Center and wondered what to do next.

Looking around for inspiration, she found a travel bag in the backseat. The accordion file contained all the necessary paperwork for a fake identity, like in the witness protection. It included a newspaper clipping from the "Want Ads" asking for nurses' aides for the Beach View Nursing Home.

The tired woman who conducted her interview was obviously desperate for a warm body to fill the spot. She hired Megan with only a cursory glance at her pseudo-references. Her bag included blue scrubs so that she could begin work the moment she got the job. She reflected that someone had been awfully confident she would pass the interview, so much so that she wondered if Nick had fixed it somehow like he had controlled the weather on the mountain.

Thanks to staff nametags, she found Ophelia easily, standing in the hallway swinging the hand of a wheelchair-bound resident who was cackling at her insistence that he dance with her. Meg had always dreaded nursing homes as dark institutions filled with the stench of death, but everyone she saw sitting around smiled or laughed, and the area around the nurses' station seemed bright and cheerful with the glow of Ophelia's joyous gyrations. Merry garlands draped the nurses' station, and a sparkling tree covered with hand-tied bows brightened a dark corner.

Ophelia saw Meg standing off to the side and bounded up to her like an excited puppy. "Hey there, girlfriend," she said enthusiastically, holding out her hand to shake. "I'm Ophelia."

"I'm Megan," she replied shyly, though she couldn't help smiling at the woman's zeal, "I just got hired."

"Welcome, welcome." Ophelia grinned. "Boy, we sure can use the help. Come on. I'll show you the ropes."

Meg had always been uncomfortable around old people, but she found herself intrigued as she saw them through Ophelia's eyes. Each one had a story, even the ones who couldn't speak, and the effusive nurses' aide knew them all. Mr. Longwood had been born two streets over and lived in a ten block radius his entire 83 years. Mr. Green had immigrated to the United States from Poland as a small child, but he still spoke with the Eastern European accent he had always heard at home. Mrs. Waller had five children she had raised in a two bedroom apartment in Brighton Beach. Ophelia gleefully warned Meg to be prepared for the mob of children and grandchildren who arrived to visit her every week. "Some of the other residents don't like it," she said. "Be ready to close doors and crank up TV's to tune out the noise."

Ophelia's favorites were Mr. McQuiddy and Mrs. Johnson. Currently living in separate rooms, they had decided to marry so that they could eat and watch TV together without disturbing their roommates. It would be the first happy celebration ever seen in a chapel usually reserved for worship and memorial services. All the staff and residents were in a tizzy about it. "You came at the right time," she said. "Next week we're going to have a wedding."

Meg discovered that in spite of Ophelia's carefree attitude, being a nurse's aide was laboriously hard work. It was obvious immediately why they had hired her so quickly. Even with her extra pair of hands, they had to work through breaks and meals to tend everyone's needs. The lifting, changing, and feeding strained her back and hours standing wore her feet out. Ophelia's enthusiasm carried the staff through it all. She danced from room to room, entering every door like a comedian bounding onstage. No one could be grumpy for long in the face of her unbridled joy.

Meg wondered where she should go when her shift ended. She checked the accordion file and found that, of course, she had a key attached to a card with an address.

The apartment was modest but clean and comfortable. Its lack of décor had obviously been intended to keep her from becoming too attached to it as a home, but a comforting framed picture of Molly and her brood, and a few colorful drawings by Bobby and his sisters attached to the refrigerator with magnets brightened the place. A note attached beside the drawings said that the subway was a much easier trip to the nursing home than driving her car.

Nick had been there.

The next morning Meg was not surprised to find that Ophelia made the same trip on the same train. "You live out here?" she asked innocently.

"I do," Ophelia replied with excitement. "Us riding in together every day? This is going to be great." She segued easily. "So Megan, do you have a family?"

"Nope, just me. How about you?"

"Oh yeah. A boy and two girls. Do you want to see their picture?"

"Please."

Ophelia pulled out a picture showing herself and three young children. "It's from the church directory."

"They're beautiful," Meg commented sincerely, "but they look like a handful."

"Yeah, they're pretty busy," she laughed, "but they keep me young."

"Where are they while you work?" She thought she should start digging a little bit.

Ophelia's trusting nature gave Meg information without any suspicion at all. "Max is in second grade this year, and Juliet is in kindergarten. Maria is only two, so I'll have to keep her in daycare for a while."

"What about your husband?" Meg asked tentatively. Children did not guarantee a live-in dad, but Ophelia wore a slender gold band on the ring finger of her left hand.

For the first time Ophelia's smile faded, and Meg felt remorse for having brought up a painful subject.

"Leon died in a construction accident two years ago, right after Maria was born."

"I'm so sorry," Meg replied.

"He was a good man," she said sadly, "and it's been hard, I'm not going to lie, but I still have the best of him in my three little angels."

"I'd like to meet them sometime," Meg commented cheerfully, hoping to return Ophelia to her jovial mood.

"What are you doing for dinner tonight?"

"The usual," Meg replied evasively.

"Why don't you come over? It's not fancy, but it's better than microwave. I'm a good cook, if I do say so myself."

"I'm a stranger to you, Ophelia. Are you sure you want me in your house? What about the children?"

"We may have just met," she replied, "but you are not a stranger. I would love for you to come."

"I can't turn that down, can I? You're the first friend I've made since I got here."

They arrived to find one of the residents ranting out of control about what idiots the employees were and yelling that he wasn't going to do anything they asked. Ophelia's summons to his room the moment they walked in the door without even the opportunity to put her things away annoyed Megan.

"Can't they wait one minute while you take off your coat and drop your purse off at your locker?" Meg said irritably.

"It's okay," Ophelia replied, "he likes me. When he gets like this they call me in to calm him down. He just needs attention, you know?" Meg trailed her in the direction of the commotion. A frazzled nurse was negotiating with a man agitated beyond reason. A large, muscular orderly nearby kept watch in case things got physical. Another young woman, a nurse's aide scarcely more than a child, tried to calm his confused roommate.

Ophelia, still in her coat, stepped right up to the bed and took the angry man's hand. "What is all this about?" she said calmly. "Mr. McGinnis, why are you causing all this ruckus?"

"Thank God you're here," he raged, "you're the only one with a lick of sense. The rest of them are incompetent idiots."

"You know that's not true. All these nice people take good care of you. Why are you being so mean to them?"

"I won't talk in front of them. You make them leave. I'll tell you what they are doing to us, but not while they're listening. They'll call me a liar. They'll say I'm crazy. I am not crazy!"

"I know you're not," she soothed. Looking at the others in the room, she said, "It's okay guys. Give us a sec." She didn't have to ask twice. They were more than happy to abandon her to face the lunatic in the bed alone.

Meg leaned against the door and tried to hear what was going on inside. The commotion had quieted, and she couldn't hear anything at all through the thick hospital door. After a very long few moments, the door opened and a smiling Ophelia came out. "You guys can go in now. He's promised he'll behave."

Ophelia walked purposefully down the hall toward the locker room, and Meg had to jog to keep up. "What did you say to him?"

"I told him the truth—that he knew these people were good people, and they took good care of him and he shouldn't treat them so bad. Then I asked him what in his life made him feel this way about people. Once he starts telling a story, he forgets all the other stuff."

"It's not fair for them to leave you alone with him. He might hurt you."

"How's he going to hurt me? He can't even sit up by himself. Besides, he wouldn't do me any harm. He and I are good friends. It makes me feel good that I am the one they call on, you know? Like I'm important, even though I'm just an aide."

"From what I've seen in two days, you are far more than just an aide."

"I want to help, you know? I can't imagine knowing I had to spend the rest of my life in a nursing home. By the time you get to us, we're your last stop, if you know what I mean. That can't be fun."

Meg spent the first couple of hours shadowing Ophelia, then, feeling more confident about the job, took on her own list of tasks. She helped distribute meals and fed residents who couldn't hold a spoon. She helped change beds and give baths. Thanks to Ophelia's tutelage, she looked past the helpless elderly people on the beds and listened to the stories. She learned what it had been like to be a little girl during the depression and to be a holocaust survivor liberated in Austria. She heard stories of New York in its heyday and how a young couple had come to the big city from a little farm town in Idaho, seeking a different kind of life. Soldiers in World War II, Korea and Vietnam. A singer from the Cotton Club in Harlem. There were so many that she could not keep them all straight, and one story spilled into the next, and into the next, and into the next. She found that at the end of the day, it was not the hard work she remembered clearly, but instead the faces of the storytellers she couldn't get out of her mind.

On the subway home, Ophelia, as cheerful as when the day began, asked Meg how she felt after her first real day on the job. "The truth is I loved it. I didn't expect to, but I really did. Like you said, it feels good to help."

"I guess we never know where we're going to find our places."

"Absolutely." Meg saw her opportunity and seized it. "It's hard work for not much pay, though. I can't imagine how you can make ends meet on this salary."

"I get by all right," Ophelia replied, but Meg noted that her smile was forced.

Ophelia lived in an apartment in an old building that had left its best days behind it. They passed door after dreary door in a hallway dark from burned out light bulbs. The last door they came to was like bright sunlight in the midst of a dismal day. A cheery Christmas wreath and *Welcome* sign dared the other bleak doors to dampen its mood. A cacophonous clatter of crashing pots and pans sounded from within.

"Sounds like Maria's making dinner again," Ophelia said with a grin.

Picking up a sealed envelope that had been shoved under the door, she went straight to the kitchen and scooped up a squirming two-year-old. Maria's cooking consisted of banging the pots and pans on the floor, or with a spoon, or with whatever she could use to make as much noise as possible. The other two children sat on the floor in the living room in front of an old TV watching a Disney Christmas cartoon, the sound loud enough to be heard over the kitchen symphony. In the midst of all it all, an old woman snored, sound asleep in a shabby, overstuffed chair, oblivious to the noise and seemingly secure that the children would not do any damage to themselves or the apartment.

Ophelia carried the little percussionist into the living room and turned down the volume on the TV. She stirred the woman in the chair and sent her home with many thanks and a twenty dollar bill.

"Her daughter must have left her to go to work. I should have been here twenty minutes ago."

When she opened her wallet, Meg could see that giving up the twenty left her wallet completely empty.

A beautiful little Christmas tree stood brave and strong in the corner, accepting with determination its mission to hold the wolves of despair at bay. It was completely covered with handmade decorations as though a Christmas spirit bomb had exploded and turned every available scrap of paper, fabric and foil into a celebration of the holiday. The popcorn garland was missing pieces here and there, probably stolen by a hungry child who recognized a new source for snack food.

Ophelia thrived on the urchins clamoring for her attention, talking to her all at once as though completely unaware that the others were there. Miraculously, she was able to filter through the conversations to pick out the highlights from each. All of this she did while turning a pound of ground beef and a box of spaghetti into dinner for five.

At first the children ignored Meg, but once she was introduced they turned their full attention on her. She backed away from them until they trapped her against the chair, and she fell back with two climbing into her lap and one sitting on the floor waiting to be picked up. Loud, boisterous and happy, they had obviously never met anyone who didn't love them absolutely.

After dinner Meg helped with the dishes, and then Ophelia offered her a cup of coffee while they chatted.

Ophelia opened the envelope from the floor by the door, glanced over it quickly and cast it aside with a sigh.

"Wow," Meg began, "you really have a full plate."

She chuckled, "I wouldn't have it any other way."

Meg felt ashamed of every minute she had spent feeling sorry for herself. "You have a great attitude."

"You would have a great attitude, too, if you were as rich as I am."

When a sleepy little voice called Ophelia away to the bedroom, Meg sneaked a look at letter she had cast aside. The landlord was threatening eviction if back rent wasn't paid within 30 days.

"You are so good with people," Meg said when she returned. "Have you ever considered getting a better paying job?"

Ophelia laughed. "You're nice to say so, but how in the world am I going to go get a better paying job when I never went to college. Besides, I love my job. If I left, who would rein in Mr. McGinnis?"

As Megan walked the three blocks to her temporary apartment, she focused so completely on what she would report that she didn't notice the hooded man walking up behind her until he grabbed her arm. The terror that squeezed her stomach gave way to butterflies as she recognized Nick's handsome face. "Stop doing that. You nearly gave me a heart attack."

He laughed. "Sorry. You were so intent on your thoughts that I couldn't get your attention any other way."

"I'm glad you're here. I don't need any more time on this one. She is the best, the very best. She deserves everything you have to throw at her—money, clothes, toys, everything."

"Tell me."

"She is a single mom raising three happy kids on less than a shoestring. She could feel sorry for herself over losing her husband, over having a hard, low paying job, or over having no time to herself, but she doesn't. She gives and gives to those people at the nursing home, and not just the patients. She keeps the staff going too with her great attitude. I know I've only watched her for a couple of days, but I can say without reservation she is the most positive, encouraging person I have ever met."

He nodded appreciatively at her enthusiasm. "That's good. Now all we have to do is decide how to help her."

"What do you mean? I told you, give her everything."

"Megan, handing people things is not always the best way to serve them. Remember the old proverb, 'Give a man a fish, he eats for a day. Teach a man to fish and he eats for a lifetime.' Ophelia does not want a handout. If she did, she would have asked before now. We need to clear a path for her that will give her a permanent solution."

"How do we do that?"

"You're the field rep, not administration. We'll work on that in the home office. In the meantime, you're ready to move on to the next stop."

"What's the hurry?"

"Christmas is coming."

"So?"

"Christmas is our deadline. It's much easier to disguise the things we do at a time of year when all sorts of mysterious gifts appear."

"I have to tell her good-bye. I can't just disappear on her after she has been so kind. I'll tell her my

71

parents called and I have to go home. But I want her to know how much I learned from her. I'll never complain about my life again."

He chuckled again. "Isn't this a great job?"

She gave in to the impulse to throw her arms around him. "Yes, thanks for picking me…" She leaned back to look him fully in the face. "Wait a minute. Is this your solution for my problems? Did someone send you a message about me?"

He smiled a knowing smile and leaned in to kiss her. Ignoring her question, he said, "Be assured we'll do right by her."

"I trust you," she replied honestly, knowing better than to push him for information he didn't want to give. "What is my next assignment?"

"Florida," he said. "Time for a warmer climate."

Chapter 9

Eddie

While the other assignment cards had been designed with beautiful, elaborate scrollwork, the one in the new accordion folder in her hotel room had no ornamentation. On the front was the name *Eddie* in simple handwritten print. Just *Eddie*. No last name, no descriptors. On the back the same scribe had written the address *Rick's Café, 111 Beachfront Ave., Destin, Florida.* A long drive from Brooklyn.

Meg drove straight through the eighteen hours between New York and Florida, leaving at one o'clock in the morning and arriving just in time for dinner. She'd take the perfect opportunity to scope out the café and see if "Eddie" was working. She pulled into a parking lot far too small for a restaurant of its size, and maneuvered her compact car into a space barely wide enough for a motorcycle. Her open door made for a tight squeeze, as sucking in her stomach swelled her chest and hunching her shoulders pushed out her backside. Finally she unwedged herself and fell back against the car, emptying the lungful of air she had been holding. The refill drained all the stress from her body and cleared her mind. Two more deep breaths of the fragrant sea air and she was ready to have a look at the beckoning beach.

The broad expanse of sand between the boardwalk and the ocean reflected a faint pink in the setting sun. Low tide. It had been years since she'd been to a Florida beach, but she knew what she would find when she walked along its edge. Sanderlings chased tiny mollusks that frantically buried themselves in the wake of the withdrawing waves. Seagrass caught around her ankles as the foamy water washed over her bare feet. Crabs skittered away from diving seagulls. Always the powerful waves washed in and out, rushing and receding as a Zen-like mantra to soothe a troubled soul.

She dragged herself away from the ocean and walked up the wood-plank stairs into Rick's Café. The décor paid homage to Casablanca, but the crowd was hardly French resistance. They lounged and chatted, nursing cheap beers and sharing pizzas and wings. The dress code was cutoffs and flip-flops. Multi-colored lights wound casually around every beam and post, and Christmas wreaths made of sea shells and dried marsh reeds hung on every door and window.

In the midst of the "Margaritaville" crowd, the waitresses flew into and out of the kitchen with dazzling speed. A lone, hunched figure carried a bus-pan bulging with the weight of stacked plates and glasses. As he cleared off the table for Megan to sit down, she spoke to him so he would look at her. Nametag: "Eddie." Bingo.

There wasn't much opportunity for a patron to speak to a busy busboy, but she watched him closely as she nursed her light beer and munched on nachos. He looked so young. He couldn't have been more than eighteen or nineteen. He was tall and thin, but he had a sweet sincere face that lit up gratefully at every "thank you". She made note that some of people tipped him directly as they left.

Meg was still working on the enormous mound of chips and salsa when she saw him pull off his apron and push quickly out the door. She couldn't move fast enough to catch him without drawing attention, so she resigned herself to finding out more the next day and flagged down the waitress for her check.

Having no idea where Eddie had gone or how to begin to look for him, Megan plugged the directions to her hotel into the GPS. Distance: .2 miles. Drive time: <5 minutes. She should have known. Didn't Nick always have everything planned to the nth degree? It was a quaint little beachside motel, a holdover from the early days of family vacations in the station wagon, but well-maintained and up-to-date, with cable TV and Wi-Fi. She dropped her bag on the bed and gave in to the magnetic force drawing her back to the beach.

The stars flickered on like someone flipping switches in a steady progression from the horizon across the sky. A few other solitary beachcombers stood silhouetted against the city lights in the distance, but most of the busy wildlife had called it a night. She veered away from the markers of a sea turtle nest, and her ears caught faint strains of music floating on the breeze. She rotated slowly, scrutinizing every inch of shoreline, and finally found its source tucked neatly in a crook of marsh grass. A young man strummed a guitar and sang softly. Eddie. She motioned to him for permission to sit, and he nodded without speaking.

The finish of the old acoustic guitar had rubbed away from years of strumming. Long pieces of string stuck out from the tuning pegs where it had been restrung but not neatly trimmed. It fit in his lap as though custom-made for that very spot, though it had certainly been in use well before he was born. Meg did not recognize the song, but she closed her eyes and let it roll over her, a duet with the crashing waves.

When he stopped singing and sat randomly plucking the strings, she finally spoke. "Thank you for letting me listen. You are really good."

"Thanks." He smiled sheepishly. "You caught me on a good day."

"I doubt that," Meg soothed. "I have a feeling you are that good every day."

He did not reply, but he sat idly strumming. She was struck again by his youthful appearance, but now, closer to him, she also felt the weight of a hard life. He might not have seen many years, but he had done enough in that time for a much older man. There was certainly a need here, but how could she get him to open up to a complete stranger?

"I saw you at the restaurant tonight, didn't I? Are you also a professional musician?" she asked, grasping for a conversation starter.

He chuckled. "Nope, although Rick's lets me play for tips some nights."

"I'll bet you do very well."

"The folks that come in there are really nice. I think they give me money because they feel sorry for me more than because they like the music."

"I doubt that," she replied, jumping into the opening he had left for her. "Why would they feel sorry for you?"

A protective wall went up between them. He was friendly, but not naïve. "I'm a young guy bussing tables, scrounging for tips wherever I can get them. It just screams 'I need help!' Don't you think?"

"Maybe so," she replied in such a way that he wouldn't feel pressed for details he obviously didn't want to give. "I'd like to hear you play and decide for myself."

"Sure. I'll be playing after my shift tomorrow night."

"Excellent. I'll be there. My name is Megan. I'm visiting from D.C."

"Nice to meet you, Megan. My name is Eddie."

Meg got to Rick's a little later the next night. Hoofing it from her hotel, she realized why the parking lot was so small, although the restaurant was full. Most people walked, many of them coming up off the beach. Eddie saw her and made a quick stop at her table. "This time order the fish and chips," he whispered. "They're a lot better than the nachos."

He was right. The fish and chips were delicious. By the time Eddie started his set, Megan sat, full and content, nursing her second beer. Before he started playing, he spoke to two girls occupying the table next to the performance platform. Their presence was noteworthy because of their ages. One looked to be in her early teens and the other couldn't have been more than six or seven. Both were too young to be sitting in a bar so late. They were most certainly part of his story.

Eddie started his set with a mix of beach songs and added in some classics by Jim Croce, Bob Dylan, and Simon and Garfunkel. Every few songs he threw in a Christmas tune, and Meg could see some of the audience mouthing the words in mute sing-along. During uncomfortable lulls in their private conversations, the patrons would turn their attention to him, nodding and raising their glasses in acknowledgement. Eddie always nodded and smiled without missing a beat.

Then he closed his eyes and began singing so softly and with such emotion, that people stopped talking and silenced their tablemates so they could

77

hear. The words to Phil Collins' "You'll Be in My Heart" sounded as though they came from Eddie's heart. Megan knew this song. She had watched Disney's *Tarzan* several times with her nephews, but she had never heard it sung like this, with so much love and truth and promise. He looked to the table where the girls sat and sang to them as if they were the only people in the room. The little one crawled into the lap of the older girl, laid her head against her shoulder and closed her eyes. The older girl locked eyes with Eddie and her mouth turned up in a slight smile. They shared something that no one else could know. Meg saw a few of the women brush away tears, and she was fighting her own.

When he came to speak to Meg after his set, she said softly, "Those girls must be your biggest fans." She hoped he would volunteer his story so that she wouldn't have to push him out of his comfort zone to get it. If her last two stops were any indication, she didn't have long and so she needed to get moving, fast.

"Just babysitting," he replied, looking their way fondly. "My folks had a thing, and I had to work so I brought them here. The owners know them, so it's all good."

"That's impressive," Meg replied curiously, "You don't often run into a young man willing to take care of his younger siblings while he is working. Or parents who would ask, for that matter."

"Hmmm," he replied, rising quickly from his chair and turning his body toward the kitchen like he was ready to run. "Got to go. Thanks for coming."

A quick getaway. Or so he thought.

Megan watched until they left, then followed them to see where they headed. There were plenty of shadows on a moonless night, so she had no problem staying out of sight as they walked down the beach away from the more populated area to a small, dark shack out of view from everything else around it. The light that came on inside flickered and danced. She couldn't see through the windows from where she was and couldn't see around her well enough to sneak through the brush and peek inside. She decided to come back in the daylight to see if she could see more from a safe distance.

Meg rose well before sunrise and set herself up in a secluded position with a beach chair and a cup of coffee. She had found binoculars in the car, and now she knew why. She saw Eddie leave for an early morning jog on the beach, return, and emerge thirty minutes later, changed into jeans and t-shirt. He trudged up a well-trod path to the road, got behind the steering wheel of an older model Hyundai and drove away. In the time Megan spent debating whether or not to go after him, he returned with a RaceTrac bag and a tray of drinks. After a while, he came out with the younger of the two girls and walked up the beach with her. She jumped and danced in the waves, stopping frequently to examine some treasure washed ashore by the friendly lapping waves of the Gulf of Mexico. They crouched with their heads together over every lucky find. Meg was moved to tears to see Eddie's tenderness and patience. Then in one fell swoop, he scooped up his little sister and planted her on his shoulders. Her yellow curls bounced as she squirmed with joy on the playful ride home.

Meg spotted no signs of any other adults.

Meg wished Nick would show up and tell her what to do. Obviously these kids had secrets, but there was no way to know who, what or why. No doubt this was why she was here, but she could make things so much worse in so many ways if she mishandled the situation. On the other hand, she could not in good conscience let it continue to exist as it was. Asking was the only way to find out what she needed to know, but not here, not now. Something told her that if she played her hand too soon they would skitter like scared rabbits before she could do them any good.

All three emerged mid-morning and walked determinedly down the beach, the older girl carrying a heavy-laden reusable grocery bag. Megan followed them at a discrete distance, using the binoculars to see when they left the beach between a collection of resort chairs and umbrellas occupied by a diverse assortment of tourists, from frolicking families and too-cool-for-words teens, to business escapees sucking in fresh ocean air before returning to their prison-in-paradise boardrooms. Fortunately, in this mini-crowd Megan could hide in plain sight and keep an eye on them from a closer vantage point.

Eddie planted the girls at a table close to the pool and took his place in the towel room, handing out, replenishing and collecting towels for resort guests. Some of the women flirted with him as he went about his job. With the younger ones he would smile and tease, but with the older ones he kept a polite distance, quickly cutting off any attempts at conversation. Meanwhile, the older sister read with the little one and pulled a drawing board out of the bag. At lunch time one of the waitresses appeared with sandwiches for the girls, after which they went for a swim, all under the watchful eyes of their brother.

He called them back to their table when he caught sight of a teenage boy looking at the older girl with a little too much interest. Megan couldn't hear what they said, but it was obvious that the girl was not happy

80

with him for taking her away from the attention, especially when he made her put her t-shirt on over her bathing suit. They leaned in close, red-faced, yelling in muffled tones, until the little girl began to cry and beg them not to fight. They stopped immediately and picked her up between them, comforting her as if they were her parents. Before long the girls settled into some afternoon math project sorting and counting Skittles. Meg was not surprised that they ate as many as they counted, but she had to wonder about the situation. The older girl was teaching the younger one, but who was teaching her?

The girls left when the lifeguards blew a four o'clock pool break. Megan felt torn between staying with Eddie and following his sisters. She decided to follow the girls, knowing that Eddie was safe where he worked and wondering what they would do when he wasn't watching them. She stayed carefully out of his view as she slipped back down to the beach.

They walked. They played. They collected beach debris and identified it with a worn looking field guide. They used another one to identify birds. A science lesson, Megan thought with admiration. Clever girl.

Eddie didn't bus tables that night, but showed up at eight to play and sing. When he paused for a break, he walked over to her table, but he was not smiling. He sat down and leaned in so that no one else could hear. "I saw you watching us all day," he growled, an impressively frightening sound from one so young. "Why?"

Megan had to think fast. "Someone has seen you around and thought you might need some help. He asked me to check up on you to see what was going on."

"Who? Who thought I needed help?"

"If he wanted you to know, he would have done it himself."

Eddie tensed like a trapped cat. "Is he here now? Is he watching us?"

"No," she answered honestly. Where was Nick when she really needed him? "Eddie, please calm down. I don't have any ulterior motives or any hidden agendas. I was truly trying to understand what is going on with your family and see if you need any help. That's all, I promise."

"What does your promise mean to me?" he asked hotly. "I don't even know you."

"That's true. Can we talk after you're done? Here on the back deck where we're close to lots of people? Hopefully I can persuade you to trust me, and maybe you'll find me a useful friend."

His eyes narrowed. "Alright," he said slowly, "after the last set. Just you. No cops."

"You have my word. The police are not involved in this in any way."

Meg picked a place on the deck that offered a quick, easy escape to the beach so that Eddie would feel more comfortable and less trapped. When he and the girls sat at the table she could see that they looked like an age progression of the same face. The little girl had the chubby cheeks of the very young and soft, bouncy yellow curls, but the same straight nose and jade green eyes. The older sister had begun to mature into the woman she would shortly be. High cheekbones defined her elegant face, the green eyes guarded but hopeful, her thick hair bronze in the transition from the younger blond to Eddie's older brown. Then of course there was Eddie, whose handsome young face did not yet have the lines that would one day reflect the weariness already showing in his version of the same green eyes.

"These are my sisters," he said with measured words, guaranteeing that he didn't reveal any more information than he felt he safely could. "Natalie and Suzanne."

"Hello, Natalie, Suzanne. I am Megan," she said, hoping her tone would relax them.

"So Megan," he began suspiciously, "tell us why you are watching us."

"I was watching you to see if you needed any help," she said, holding her palms up as if offering them a gift. "Some of the folks around here have seen you all together, seen how hard you are working, Eddie, and how the girls come in with you until so late, and they have wondered what your story is."

"What does that have to do with you?"

"One of them, he wants to be anonymous, asked me if I'd look into it for him. So I have."

"You're not a very good spy," Eddie said wryly, "I saw you coming miles away."

She had to laugh, "I can't argue with that. He certainly didn't ask me because of my cat-like stealth."

"Then why? Why you? Why us?"

Megan tried to hold Eddie's eyes without looking away, but in the face of his intense glare she had to glance over at Natalie and Suzanne. Suzanne had fallen asleep in Natalie's arms, sucking absently on the comforting thumb in her mouth. Natalie had squeezed her eyes shut, but when she opened them they were not cold, hard stones of anger like Eddie's. They were sad and scared and threatening to overflow with tears.

Maternal urges Meg had never felt before kicked in all at once and slammed her so hard she fell back in her chair. In that moment she knew she would do anything she could to help these children. Anything, except for the fact that she had no idea what that thing should be. "Guys," she said, "I really just want to help."

Eddie and Natalie must have seen the change in her, because in the space of one breath they sat back in their chairs and relaxed. "I believe you, though I'm not sure why," Eddie replied with an affirmative nod from Natalie, "What do you want to know?"

"Who are you? Where are you from?"

"Those are not good questions, Megan," he replied with astonishing maturity, "I'm not going to tell you our last name or where we're from. Try again."

Meg sighed. "Fair enough. How did you come to be here? Where is your family?"

Again Natalie nodded, encouraging her brother to tell the story. "Our parents were killed in a crazy boating accident. Just a fun day with the neighbors and they never came home. They had no wills, and nobody wanted all three of us, so they were going to split us up." He gently stroked a blond curl off Suzanne's sleeping face. "Our aunt Judy jumped in real quick for Suzanne with those cute blond curls and chubby cheeks and all. My dad's brother and his wife were a lot older, and they never wanted children, but they were going to fulfill their family obligation and take on Natalie. Me, well, none of them wanted a seventeen year old boy, so I was just going to be an unpleasant burden for somebody.

"After the funeral, when they came to get us we asked for time to say goodbye privately. I grabbed the keys, threw the girls in Mom's car and left. I never slowed down, never looked back, never even thought where I was going. I just drove in a straight a line as best I could, on back roads and highways, until I finally felt safe to stop. I sat in a rest stop and thought things through. We weren't going back no matter what, and anybody we would turn to for help would send us back right away. I knew we needed money, and I didn't have much, although Mom's purse was still in the car. I took the cash from her wallet, but I could never use her credit cards or they would find us. I did know her ATM pin and used it just once to get gas and cash, then left her purse in the bathroom at the gas station. I figured that if we were going to have to live outside, it had better be a place where that would be warm year 'round. Florida was south, and I knew my way, and it was in the opposite direction from the way they would be looking for us. So here we are." His anger was gone, his expression unreadable.

Meg didn't know what to say, but she knew she had to think carefully about her reply. This was no occasion for a flippant 'Gee whiz' or an insincere 'Boy that's tough.' This was a lot of pain and an incredible act of trust to share it. "How long?" she croaked.

"Two years."

"You've been on your own for two years with these little girls?"

He exchanged affectionate glances with Natalie. "We've been on our own for two years with one little girl," he said. "I could never have done it if Natalie and I weren't a team."

"How old are you?" Megan directed at Natalie.

"Fourteen," she replied quietly.

"Fourteen," Megan whispered. "And how old are you, Eddie?"

"I'm nineteen," Eddie replied with a grin, "things got a lot easier when I got legal."

"And Suzanne?"

"She's six. Sometimes at the beginning she would cry for Mom, but we did our best for her and now she's okay. Mostly."

"That makes me sad," Megan said honestly, thinking for the first time about how her own mother must have felt when she disappeared. "There must be someone who is looking for you."

"Only because they're supposed to." His agitation flared again. "There is no way we're going back to that. Wherever we go, we go together. We're all we've got."

"You're right," Meg choked out. She couldn't let this get out of hand. She had to stay with them, had to see this through. She brushed the tears off her cheeks. "What about school?"

"We're home schooling," he replied.

"Home schooling Suzanne," Meg replied, "What about you two?"

"I was done anyway," Eddie said flatly, "I was a good student and got more out of my time in high school than most people who stay to graduate."

"And Natalie?"

"I'm doing okay," she spoke for herself for the first time. "I read a lot."

"But two years ago you were only twelve. You haven't even finished eighth grade."

"I know, but I'm a really good reader, and Eddie is really smart. He uses the computer at the resort to run off the curriculum information for what I'm missing. I bet I know more than most of the kids who've stayed in school."

Meg decided that this was not the discussion to be having. School was certainly the least of their problems. Better to be encouraging and keep their trust. "How have you been living? How have you kept a roof over your heads?"

"We've lived in that house on the beach for a long time," Eddie said. Now that he could see she wasn't going to dial 911 as soon as she heard their story he warmed to the telling. "It's been a great location. Down the beach I work in the resort, up the beach I work at Rick's. They all love the girls, so we eat pretty well." He was proud, proud that he had found such a great place, proud that he had taken such good care of his sisters, proud that he had done it all without help.

"But there isn't any electricity."

"We don't need it, do we, Nat?"

She shook her head in agreement. "Everything we need, we can get at the resort."

"Hasn't somebody noticed you? Hasn't somebody tried to turn you in?"

"Naw," Eddie said. "That place is so big we don't show up on their radar at all."

"Well then," Meg said, unsure of what else to say, "I guess you've got it all figured out."

"Yep," Eddie replied, "We're doing okay."

Megan knew they weren't okay. They needed a roof over their heads that wouldn't blow away in an ocean storm. They needed real beds with clean sheets and a working bathroom. They needed school so that they didn't have to spend the rest of their lives in a shack on the beach. They needed love and security and a home. What they didn't need was to be separated like lost pieces of a puzzle. What was the solution to their problem?

"We've got to go," Eddie said and Natalie nodded her agreement. They stood up and Eddie took the sleeping Suzanne in his arms, cradling her against his chest. "Thanks for caring, Megan, but really, we've got this."

She sat listening to the waves after they disappeared into the darkness. A shadow blocked the light coming from behind her and two strong hands squeezed her shoulders.

Nick.

"Were you eavesdropping on our conversation?" she asked casually, though there was nothing casual about the way she felt when he touched her.

"Not at all," he replied, smiling. "That's why you're here. I just listened to the music and ate some fish and chips. So what's the story?"

"They need help, Nick, and I don't think they realize how badly they need it."

"Remember, I told you that was the primary motivation for our work. Helping people in desperate situations who won't otherwise ask for help." He held out his hand to her. "Walk with me and tell me their story."

Instead of slogging through the loose sand like most people, Nick walked with easy, sure steps, leading Meg effortlessly to the hard packed sand right next to the water. They slipped off their shoes and strolled up the beach holding hands. Meg lost herself in the telling of the tale, and Nick listened thoughtfully, as always. "So Eddie is treading water as hard as he can trying to keep them together, but he can't keep it up forever, and I'm afraid of what will happen when he loses control of the situation."

Nick did not comment immediately, but continued leading her up the beach. She was learning that he often needed time to reflect on what she told him, so she gave over her consciousness to the world all around, calmed by the vastness of the sea and the invisible horizon she knew hung in the distance. The waves washed over her feet, and when the tide receded it took her stresses and concerns out with it. Deep breathing brought with it the fragrance of the salty surf, and the sea breezes blew her hair into wild, free waves around her face and shoulders.

Nick stopped, pulled her into his arms, and caressed the hair from her face. "We can help them," he said softly.

"How?" Megan asked, trying to see his face in the darkness.

"You know I can't tell you." He, kissed her lightly. "Just know that we'll take care of it. Those kids won't spend Christmas in that shack. I promise."

She wrapped her arms around his neck, pulling him down to her. "I believe you," she whispered. He kissed her as she wanted him to, deeply and passionately, until she had no breath left. "Please don't leave me," she murmured.

"I don't want to, believe me," he replied, hugging her to him as though he would pull her inside his body. "But I can't. Someday soon we'll stay together, I promise."

"Another promise?" she teased. "Those are some big words. I hope you can follow through."

"I intend to," Nick replied, kissing her again. "You will see that I am a man of my word." He paused. "But now it is time to move on."

"So quickly? What will they think when I disappear on them?"'

"That you are a tourist like all the others who come and go."

"I guess I should trust you about that. You seem to have everything else under control."

"Now you are learning," he said with a grin.

Chapter 10

Dan

Nick left her at the door of her motel room as always, vanishing before she could turn around and say goodbye. Inside she found the ever present accordion file with her mission. The new card was more ornate than Eddie's but still had a masculine feel to it. *Dan Greene* in Atlanta, Georgia.

The drive from Destin to Atlanta gave her plenty of time to reflect on her new assignment. Dan Greene was a lawyer, and she had been put in his office as a temp. When she checked into her hotel, she found a business suit in the closet, a perfect fit, of course, and everything else she needed to look professionally appropriate. Unfortunately she had to be there by 8AM, and she dropped into the bed minutes before 1. She tossed and turned, restless and uneasy in yet another strange bed in another strange city. In the foggy state between waking and sleeping, she felt as though she nestled against a warm body, in strong, protective arms, and she slipped into a deep, restful sleep.

Surprisingly refreshed, Meg woke easily and left in plenty of time to find the law offices of Howell, Rubenstein and Greene. The top of the modern glass tower was obscured by low hanging December clouds, which threatened to drop snow in the unusually cold Georgia morning. When she got off the elevator the windows that wrapped the outside of the office suite offered no view of the city since white mist completely blocked them. She had the funny sense of being on top of Mount Olympus, the home of the gods far above the lives of the common people below. In spite of the early hour, the staff already bustled about with busy purpose. The receptionist, Deena, greeted her warmly and hopped up to lead her with friendly, welcoming conversation to Dan Greene's office. "When we got in this morning he was asleep on his desk," she said confidentially. "We think he must have stayed all night. Bad timing for Grace's father to die, but what're you going to do?"

"Grace?"

"His administrative assistant," she answered, indicating the sizable work station covered with piles of files outside the large double doors.

Panic threatened to explode from Meg's stomach and spew coffee and banana muffin out all over the expensive carpet. She knew how to staple, punch holes and run a copier, but she was hardly a trained secretary. With a deep breath she steadied herself on the desk.

Deena comforted her with a gentle hand on her arm. "Don't worry." She smiled. "He's a real teddy bear to work for. He's a killer in court, but he's one of the kindest people I've ever known in my life. That's why he let Grace go without question, in spite of this huge caseload and all the preparation he needs for his hearings next week. Anything you can do will be better than no help at all." Seeing someone else come off the elevator to be greeted, she rushed back to her desk, leaving Meg to pull herself together and act like a competent administrative assistant.

She knocked lightly on the imposing door. When no reply came, she cracked it open and peeked in.

The man behind the desk lifted his head and rubbed the sleep out of his eyes. His hair looked charmingly mussed from his napping face down in a large legal tome. "Yes," he said in a hoarse morning voice that desperately needed a cup of coffee.

Meg's heart filled with immediate sisterly affection. "I'm your secretarial temp," she said kindly, "how about I start you off with a cup of coffee? What do you take in it?"

"That would be awesome. I usually have milk and sugar, but today you'd better bring it black," he replied, combing his fingers through his hair. "Thanks."

Meg followed the aroma of freshly brewed coffee to a workroom with multiple pots sitting ready for a busy day. She guessed the mug monogrammed *DG* belonged to her new boss. The remains of his all-nighter lay as sediment in the bottom. She rinsed it, wiped it out and filled it with hot, dark, liquid energy.

"Wow, thanks a lot," he said, pushing the litter of papers around on his desk until he uncovered the coffee-stained coaster. "You've already earned your paycheck, and we haven't even started working yet." He held out his hand. "I'm Dan Greene."

"Megan O'Riley." She took his hand.

"A fine Irish name," he said with a smile.

"Yes, it is."

"Okay, Megan O'Riley, are you a legal secretary?"

"I'm afraid not. Just a 'secretary' secretary."

"No offense, but the legal experience would have helped. Still, there is plenty for you to do, and you look pretty smart," he grinned flirtatiously. The coffee was working its magic. His professional persona appeared, bringing to mind imagined juries melting like butter in his hands. He picked up a sizable stack of letter-sized sheets of paper clipped into several different documents. "These are depositions for the cases I am working on. I need for you to go through them and proofread very carefully. I don't trust the spelling and grammar check on the computer. Highlight anything you see wrong or you think might be wrong, and I'll check them. Once they're proofed we need to make the corrections and make multiple copies." He looked at the mess on his desk and sighed. "I'd better go home and clean up before I plow into this landfill again. Work on the documents while I'm gone, and we'll see where we stand when I get back."

"Got it," Meg replied to the empty space where Dan Greene had been standing. In her other life, her real life, the nightmare life that she had left for world travel, she was an editor. She might not be much of a legal secretary, but she was a heck of a proofreader. And she was fast.

She was really, really fast. When he returned an hour later, she had plowed through the two hundred pages he had left her and sorted through the mess on his desk, sorting it into neat, obvious piles without moving anything too far from where she'd found it.

"Excellent," he said, accepting the proofread depositions, sprinkled generously with orange highlighter lines. "See, I knew the computer had missed a lot of mistakes." He had showered and shaved away the adorable little-boy-who-just-woke-up appearance. She felt that she had seen the true Dan Greene that morning, probably more than people who had known him much longer, but she understood that he was back in charge and ready to work.

"Yes, it did," she replied.

When she came back from fetching him another cup of coffee, this time with the milk and sugar he preferred, he had removed the jacket of his double-breasted suit and rolled up the sleeves of his starched white button-down. Energy radiated from his body. She readied herself like a racehorse to keep up with his machine-gun-fire pace.

"Okay," he said, "excellent job with the proofreading. Do you make corrections, too?"

"I do."

"Great. I'm almost done proofing. I'll let you go into the file on the computer and fix them. One more proof after that, and we'll send them to the copy room."

"I can make copies."

"Thanks, but you are obviously a resource better used here than there, legal secretary or not." He gave a heavy sigh. "This stack is contracts. Our client claims that the other party falsified the dates on their contracts for this downtown property to look like they superseded his. We need to find evidence of that. How do you feel about a records search?"

"Not as good as proofreading, but if you tell me what I'm looking for, I'll give it a shot."

"Better than a shot I hope, but it's not hard. I need older copies of the contract to prove they changed the dates. I'm sure they covered their tracks in every way they could think of, so we have to think of ways they didn't."

"Where did they have to be filed?" Editors also knew a bit about contracts. Multiple copies, multiple recipients.

"Good question. Real estate broker, courthouse, building permit office…"

"What about insurance?"

"Insurance," he nodded thoughtfully, "good idea. Check to see who the insurance was with. They may have changed those records, too, but some secretary could have an original copy in a file somewhere."

"They'll hide it."

"If we can catch them unawares, we can serve a subpoena before they have a chance." He took a breath and looked her full in the face. "Are you sure you're not a legal secretary?"

She smiled with satisfaction. "Nope, but I have a bit of business experience."

"Good for me," he said and went back to his work.

Fortunately, most of the contract information was public record, and all the records were available in the computer data banks. All Dan had to do was call to get her the password and she was in. She worked through the morning without a break until he sent her for fifteen minutes down time and more coffee for them both. While she sat in the break room she realized she had completely forgotten her reason for being there. He needed her help so badly, maybe she was his gift. No, it didn't work that way. She had better start keeping her eyes and ears open for hints.

Hint number one was waiting when she returned to her desk. A young woman with two young children peering out from behind her legs stood looking presumptuously at the papers on the desk. "May I help you?" she asked formally.

"Hi," The woman held out her hand. "I'm Debbie, Dan's sister."

"Oh," Meg relaxed, "Hi. I'm Megan. I'm temping for him while Grace is away."

"Whew, that's good. He really needs it. He's lost without Grace." She scooped the little ones out from behind her. "This is Ethan and Emily. They want to visit Uncle Dan."

"He's awfully busy," Meg replied hesitantly. "Let me tell him you're here."

"No need. If we ask, he won't let us in," she said, ruefully. "Come on kids." She opened the door and let them through like monkeys escaping a cage.

"Deb," Dan hardly had time to stand before the children barreled into him like little bulldozers. Ethan jumped into the chair and started swiveling around, his five-year old legs, dangling well above the floor. Three-year-old Emily had grabbed onto one of her uncle's legs and rode his foot as he stepped across the room to hug his sister. "This is a surprise," he said, the stress of interruption evident in his voice, "what's up?" He reached down without looking and Emily grabbed on, further fitting the monkey metaphor. He pulled her up squealing and giggling, until her chubby little arms had his neck in a stranglehold embrace.

"I knew it would be harder for you to turn me down in person," Debbie said, looking up at her brother. She was at least a foot shorter and several years younger, but there was no question who was in charge.

"Turn you down?"

"The party? On Friday?"

"Right. Sorry, Deb, no can do."

"Danny…"

"No, seriously, look at all this mess. I'm due in court on Monday. Monday, Deb. As in three days from today. I'll be pulling all nighters every night."

"Nope, sorry. Can't accept that." She crossed her arms to make her intentions clear. "You will be at this party, and you will be charming."

"Why does this matter?" Dan pleaded while little Emily played with his hair. "It's Greg's office party. Why am I going, anyway?"

"Because Cindy will be there."

"And this matters to me because?"

"You know why."

"You keep trying to throw us together, but it never takes. She doesn't talk. How am I supposed to get to know a woman who doesn't talk?"

"She does talk, but you intimidate her. Six-foot two and gorgeous in starched shirts and pinstripes, versus computer geek more comfortable online than face-to-face."

"Intimidating? Megan is not intimidated, are you?" He looked past his sister to Meg standing in the door, watching the scenario play out with great amusement.

Like a deer caught in the headlights of an oncoming car, Meg panicked. She had not expected to be brought into their family squabble. She swallowed and said, "Not at all." Her tone did not convince Dan's determined sister.

"She's lying."

"Seriously? After you saw me asleep on my desk, drooling on the book I slept on, hair sticking up like Buckwheat, you find me intimidating?"

Meg chuckled. "When you put it that way, no, I guess I don't."

"See?" said Dan, satisfied, "not intimidating. Cindy simply doesn't want to talk to me."

"Stop it. She's perfect for you. This is a great opportunity for you guys to get to know each other, because you won't know anyone else." She grinned mischievously.

"Great." He moved back around his desk and lifted his squirming nephew out of his chair. "I can't, Deb. No time."

"You've never got time," Debbie said. "That's why you have no life."

With surprising strength, Ethan pushed his uncle back into the chair, and then climbed into his lap. He held Dan's face firmly between his hands and captured his eyes. "Uncle Dan, you have to come to this party."

Amused and indulgent, Dan played along. "Why is that, Master Jedi?"

"Because it is going to be all boring grown-ups. If you don't come I won't have anyone to play with."

"What about Emily?"

Ethan's expression of scorn was so adult that Dan could hardly keep from laughing out loud. "She's a baby and a girl. She doesn't know about Star Wars or video games or anything. I asked Santa to bring you blaster pistols, but they won't be here before the party. We'll have to play with the light sabers."

Debbie smirked. Emily had crawled into Dan's lap next to Ethan. That was the reason she had brought the children. He was powerless to resist them. He looked to Meg for a reprieve and found none.

"Fine," he said, resigned. "I'll come. But I'm playing video games with Ethan, not making a love connection with Cindy. Now, if you're going to steal a whole night from me, you have to get out so I can work."

"Done." As she left, she addressed Meg, "Make sure he leaves the office on time tomorrow. Six o'clock."

"Six o'clock?" Dan whined like a child.

"Six. O. Clock," Debbie replied emphasizing each syllable. "Make sure," she repeated to Meg and then blew out with the children like the passing of a tornado.

Dan looked up at Meg standing in the door of his office and shook his head. "She is such a brat. She was born like that—bossy and demanding. Even Mom and Dad have no resistance to her witchy powers."

"But you're going to do it."

"Of course I'm going to do it. I said I would, and I always keep my word. But I'm not going to like it, and I'm not going to take up with Greg's sister."

"Cindy is your brother-in-law's sister?" Meg asked, understanding creeping in.

"Yes, she is. And we have nothing in common. They keep pushing and pushing but it never works. Never." He sighed, releasing his exasperation. "Enough of that. Back to work."

"Okay." Meg felt that she had better help him get his work done or she, too, would endure the wrath of Debbie.

As the day wore on it became obvious he had forgotten that she was only a temp. She found the insurance information he had asked for and ran over to the courthouse with the request for a subpoena, only to find the office had closed minutes before.

Meg wondered if Nick had known what she was getting into with this job. The others had been so calm and easy. Beautiful mountains and paintings, beautiful beach and music. The nursing home had been physically hard work, but not stressful, not like this. This was more like her job had been before everything had happened, back when she had her own office and her own administrative assistant.

No one left at five o'clock, the official end of the day, but secretaries and lawyers disappeared one-by-one until only Meg and Dan were left. She was organizing the desk into manageable piles when an older woman standing silently by the receptionist's desk startled her. Her clothes were well-worn but clean, her dark hair streaked with gray. Sad, weary eyes prevented Megan from saying that the office was closed. Obviously this woman knew the office was closed.

"May I help you?" Meg asked kindly.

"Mr. Greene said he'd see me if I came after work," she replied.

"May I say who is calling?"

Before the woman could answer, Dan strode from his office. "Hello, Ava," he said warmly, without any indication that her appearance was inconvenient. "Thank you for coming."

"I appreciate your seeing me," she replied, looking around. "I know this is outside your regular hours."

"These days I don't have any regular hours." He chuckled. "Come on in and let's talk."

Meg's curiosity got the best of her, but she waited until Dan ushered his guest out to ask questions. He returned to find her staring at him, her brow furrowed.

"Debbie introduced us," Dan explained. "Ava's grandchildren go to school with Ethan. Their mom's been arrested for possession and prostitution, and DFACS is threatening to put them in foster care. Ava and her husband want custody."

"That seems like a no brainer."

"Not as easy as it sounds. The mother is not their daughter. The father is their son. He's missing in action, and since they're not married, the case is a tough sell."

"How are the kids?"

"Happier now," he responded. "It hasn't taken very long for them to respond to being in a loving, stable home. I'll do anything I can to keep them there.

Their hearing is next week, also, and if we don't get it done, the court will take the kids before Christmas."

Meg's heart melted at the passion and sincerity flashing in his red-rimmed eyes. "What can I do?"

"Megan, you are a gift from God," Dan's smile melted her heart even more. "I was desperate to have enough help to handle this case and the other. If you can follow through with the records search and document prep for the real estate case, I'll go out to the jail tomorrow to try and persuade the mom to sign papers giving over custody."

"Is that going to be a problem?"

"Ava and Russell haven't exactly been close with Cheryl. They blame her for luring their son to the dark side and have displayed significant moral outrage at her lifestyle. She thinks they look down on her, and she doesn't want them influencing the way her children feel about her."

"She's worried about what the children think, and she acts like that?"

"Yeah, well, drug-fried brains."

"Right. Do you think you can persuade her?"

"I'm going to try. You keep working, and I'll go out there first thing."

Megan got to work at seven the next morning, prompting comment by some of the other lawyers, who asked if she would be interested in a real job. She smiled and said, "Thanks but I've got all I can handle right now." She drank black coffee and blocked out all other noise and activity while she focused on the work. Those children needed to be with their grandmother. She would do all of Dan's work if she had to so that he could make that happen.

Minutes before noon he rushed into his office and dropped into the chair behind his desk. Meg followed him in with a cup of coffee and closed the door to block out nosy eavesdroppers. "So?"

Dan leaned forward and rubbed his eyes with the heels of his palms. "I got the signature."

"You were gone for hours. What happened?"

"Cheryl is not exactly a pleasant person under the best of circumstances—not that I've ever seen her under good circumstances—but in jail and in the throes of withdrawal, she is feral. All I had to do was mention Ava and Russell, and she threw a fit of impressive proportions. I didn't know if she was going to bite me or claw me or what. I was about to knock for the guard to get me out quickly, but she switched to hysterical crying and starting pawing at me like a puppy. This went on for over an hour."

"Why did you put up with it, Dan? Why didn't you just get out? You were dealing with a crazy person. Reasonable behavior was never going to be on the agenda."

"I wanted this to happen. Those kids finally have something good going on, and Ava told me that she and Russell are in for the long haul. If they get put into the system, they could be separated, moved around, or worse, have no home at all and wind up in a shelter or group home. They need to be with their grandparents who love them."

"And you got it."

"I got it."

"Now what?"

"I need to run it down to the court to file before the weekend and get it done before the holiday. Will you call Ava and Russell to meet me there?"

"Of course."

"How is the rest going?"

"It's going fine. I'm stacking it on your desk as I get done."

"Thanks, Meg. You're a lifesaver."

After taking care of Ava's day in court, Dan was barely back in the office before Meg did as Debbie had instructed her, making sure he left the office by six o'clock. "Can you work this weekend?" he asked like he was asking for a play date instead of two days of slave labor.

She nodded.

"Thanks," He put a hand on her shoulder. "really, thanks."

She smiled, thinking Debbie was not the only one with potent powers of persuasion. "No problem."

Saturday morning she went in a little later, arriving at nine with two large coffees from Starbucks. Dan already sat at his desk, wearing glasses she had not seen in the two previous days. He took them off and rubbed his eyes when she came in. "Hey," he said, "thanks for the coffee."

"Sure. How was the party?"

"I was surprised, and I am not often surprised. I did what I said I would. I hid in the basement playing with the kids until they went to bed. Deb was right, of course. I didn't know anyone but Cindy, so she and I sat in the corner like wallflowers while everyone else drank heavily. She talked this time–I had to pry it out of her, but she did talk–and it turns out we do have a few things in common. I should have known a computer geek would know *Star Wars* and *Star Trek*. She even knew my more outdated favorites like *Battlestar Gallactica* and *X-Files*. She likes romantic period pieces, too. I have no stomach for them—Jane Austen and such—but we found a good bit of common ground."

"That's good."

"Kept the party from being a total bust, for me anyway."

"Are you going to see her again?" Meg had begun to suspect why she was there.

"Don't know. No time to worry about that now." With that, the subject was dismissed.

By Sunday afternoon exhaustion had her dragging. Dan called her into his office to send her home. "You look wiped out," he said. "Sorry. Guess you didn't know what you were getting into when you took this job."

"It has been harder than I expected," she confessed, "but I have enjoyed working with you."

"Me, too." He paused. "Grace sent an e-mail. She'll be back tomorrow, so I guess you'll be out of a job. I'm sorry for that."

"Not to worry," Meg replied sincerely. "Hopefully I can enjoy a few days off before I take on another one. And the holidays are coming up fast. Funny how that happens when you don't have children to remind you hourly that Santa is coming."

"I have Ethan and Emily to remind me."

Meg thought about her nephews. "Kids make all the difference."

"Yep. I don't know that Santa is going to deliver those laser blasters. I'd better buy a backup pair just in case." He smiled and held out his hand. "I can never repay you for your work these few days, but I can give you a great reference. Make sure you have them call me whenever you need one."

"Thanks, Dan. Hopefully we will meet again. Happy holidays."

"You, too."

A familiar hooded figure waited, leaning against her car in the skyscraper's parking garage. "You look exhausted," he commented. "I prescribe dinner and bed for you."

"Is that an offer?"

"For dinner," he teased. "I love Southern food. I can't resist fried chicken and pecan pie."

"You know a place?"

"I know a place."

The unobtrusive little restaurant was packed to overflowing, but somehow Nick got a table right away ahead of others waiting lined up on the street. She laughed at the exaggerated way he made over each bite of fried chicken and mashed potatoes and flushed at his almost sexual ecstasy savoring every bite of the pecan pie. His antics charmed the staff, and he praised their work until they blushed with pride. Meg marveled at his magical way with people.

He saw her back to her hotel after dinner and up to her room. When the door closed behind him, his playful mood darkened. "Meg," he said, "this next job is a tough one, but it is your last for a while."

Something in his voice made the hair on her arms stand at attention like so many soldiers ready for battle. "Tough, how?" she asked suspiciously.

He took her hand and intertwined their fingers. Pulling her close, he kissed her as she had longed for him to since their first kiss, a million miles away and a hundred years before. Could it really have been only a few weeks?

"I've got to go," he said sadly, releasing her and moving quickly to the door. Again she had the feeling he was leaving before he lost the willpower to go. How she wished he would change his mind and stay.

When the door shut behind him, she went to turn on the television and fill the lonely, empty room with noise. Another elegantly illuminated card lay on top of the TV.

Meg gasped when she saw the name. *Amy Roberts. Washington D.C.*

Her boss's wife.

She was going home.

Chapter 11

Amy

Meg checked out of the hotel and went to her car. This time the bag in the car was the one she had left in England when Nick spirited her away. On the front seat sat her very own purse with the keys to her very own apartment in Georgetown.

Will the apartment still be mine? Will they have given me up for lost or dead and rented it out to somebody else? My clothes, my things—will they still be there? I have been gone for months. What will my parents say when they see that I am fine but didn't call? My former friends and colleagues—what will they do when they see me? What is the worst they can do? What is the best I can hope for? How will this ever be alright?

She turned up the radio as loud as she could stand it and merged onto the interstate for the long, long drive from Atlanta to DC. She tried different types of music on different stations, tried listening, tried singing, and even tried talk radio, hoping she would be so aggravated that it would put everything else out of her mind. It all worked for a while, but not for long. She managed to get all the way to North Carolina before she had to make a pit stop at the state welcome center. When she got back to the car, her emotions broke over her in waves, each one carrying a little more of her resolve away. She leaned against the steering wheel, and she gave in to the grief and fear that she had lived with since that terrible night.

A kind hand rubbed her back to soothe her. Nick sat in the passenger seat. She hadn't even heard the door open. "Nick," she uttered, barely intelligible, "I can't. I can't go back. I can't."

Nick continued to rub her back, silently allowing her to cry herself out. Finally, when she was quiet, he asked her, "What is it that you think you have done?"

"You know what I did. You've known all along."

"I have, but I've been waiting for you to say it."

"I lost control, okay?" she spat the words at him, "I lost control and I ruined—no *demolished*—the lives of everyone I care about and a few more that I don't even know!"

"Meg," he said calmly, "that is not the whole story."

"No, but it is my part in it. The most awful, horrible part."

"Yours was not the true crime."

"It was true enough. It wasn't my place to throw it out there for everyone to see. My friend trusted me, and I betrayed her trust."

"How?" he asked evenly.

"You know how," she choked out. The pain of it was too much for her to bear. A fist had grabbed her heart and squeezed so that every beat felt like it would be her last. She could only take quick, shallow breaths. The inside of the car began to wave and break into pieces like a Dali painting.

Nick's firm grip on her arm drew her back. "Meg," he said, "tell me what you are thinking. How do you remember it?"

"My boss, Richard, was having an affair with my best friend, Sue. He had a ritzy apartment for her where they could meet whenever he could manage it— which was a lot, by the way. Lunches, nights when he said he was working late, mornings before work. There were lots of times and lots of excuses. I covered for them when his wife came in. The thing that worried me the most was that Sue was truly in love with him. She wanted to marry him. He said he wanted it, too, but I knew he would never leave his wife. Everybody knew he would never leave his wife. He has a family, for God's sake, two sons and a daughter, and they are young children. But he said whatever it took to get her in bed, and she believed it all.

"It was the annual company Christmas party. We were all there, families and everybody, but no one else knew what I knew. No one else had to pretend that everything was okay. No one else had to watch their public displays of affection, them figuring since I knew there was no reason to hide it from me. How about just common decency? How about I didn't want to see it no matter what? Particularly when we were all at the office late, I had seen things I would be embarrassed to watch on television. At the party they were playing a game, trying to touch each other as many ways as possible without tipping off his wife, and Sue kept looking at me and smiling as if I was in on the joke. He winked at me…winked at me! My fury rose up until I thought my head would explode. A person should never act on impulse in such a state of mind, but then, in that condition I had no filter on my thoughts or my mouth.

"I walked up to his table, plopped myself down in his lap and proceeded to ask him why he was treating my friend the way he was, and did he really intend to leave his wife and marry her? His wife was sitting right there. Sitting. Right. There. In my numb, morally outraged haze I wasn't even aware of her. Instantly, the whole place went cold and silent as a morgue. Icicles formed on the chandeliers. The flowers on the tables wilted in the plunging temperature. He dumped me off his lap and tried to grab his wife before she could escape. She ran, literally *ran*, out the door and drove off in her big white Mercedes. He yanked me off the floor and pushed his face into mine yelling, 'What have you done?'"

Meg tried to rub the memory out of her eyes, but it burned there as brightly as the day it happened. Her voice was barely audible when she said, "His face was beet-red, and the veins in his temples were throbbing. Sue's face was ashen, and she seemed to have aged twenty years in the seconds it took me to utter one devastating sentence. Not only had I, her best friend, violated her confidence, but when she saw how he acted toward his wife, she knew she'd been played the fool. Now she was betrayed and humiliated, and her shame had been exposed in front of everyone we knew. If I had stripped off all of her clothes and left her naked in front of them she would have been less devastated. How do you even apologize for something like that? 'I'm sorry?' That hardly covers it, does it? The next week her parents had to check her into psychiatric hospital so she wouldn't commit suicide."

The words had come out in such a painful rush Megan had to pause to catch her breath.

"His wife divorced him and took him for everything she could get, an exorbitant settlement of child support and living expenses, including the mortgage on their ridiculously expensive house while she lives there with the children. He had to take on some very vocal investors to keep the business afloat, and Richard Roberts is not a man who likes to be told what to do. He would be happy to see my lifeless body hanging from a tree with my eyes pecked out by a bunch of nasty crows, and all the others would help him tie the noose. You want me to go back there?"

Nick still sat in silence, his expression unreadable.

Now that the dam had burst, Meg couldn't stop talking. It all spilled out like a river unleashed. "He laid off half of our staff and put over fifty people out of work. Fifty people with families and mortgages and car payments and bills, all unemployed just like that. All because of me. The miracle is that they didn't try to kill me when they had the chance. In some ways I wish they had, but maybe letting me live with the shame is a greater punishment."

"You thought to end that shame on your own. There on the cliffs, you planned to make it all go away," Nick said quietly.

"I hoped fate would take a hand and let the storm blow me out into the sea. It would be done now if you hadn't been there to save me. Everyone would have been better off."

"I don't believe that, and neither do you."

"How can you be so kind to me when you know what I have done? What kind of person I am?" The tears overflowed again.

He was quiet for so long that she looked up to see if he had left. He hadn't. He sat in the same position, perfectly still and unfazed, his eyes fixed on her. There was no judgment in his gaze, only kindness and compassion. "Meg," he began, "the crime is not yours."

"How can you say that? I ruined all of those lives."

"No, you didn't. Richard Roberts is the one who created the devastation. You could not have betrayed a secret if there was no secret to tell."

"What about Sue? He may have deserved what he got, but she didn't."

"That is also untrue. She made her own decision. She chose to have an affair with a married man."

"And his wife? His children? Did they deserve what it did to their lives?"

"No, of course not. But again, that was not your doing. You may have revealed it, but he was the one having the affair. He and your friend, who is a grown woman, are more than capable of accepting responsibility for their own actions."

"Still..."

"Go home, Meg. Things have played out up there in ways you did not foresee. See what is really going on. Purge your demons and get on with your life."

"Are you saying there is good that's come out of what I've done?"

He cupped her face in his hand and held her eyes with his. "That is precisely what I'm saying." He kissed her lightly. "And now there is more good for you to do." He got out of the car. "I'll see you up there." He closed the door and vanished.

Meg was not completely convinced by his arguments, but his presence had calmed her. She pulled back onto the highway and set out resolutely to finish her task. She hoped it would be her last. She hoped Nick would spirit her away when it was over, that he would take her back to his house and wrap her in his arms in front of the fireplace and let distance drive away all of the horrible memories as it had before.

For the entire long, hard day, ten interstate hours she rode the waves of her emotions from despair to acceptance to despair to acceptance but ultimately despair, in spite of Nick's encouragement. She hit the tail end of rush hour traffic on the Beltway and then crept and crawled through traffic lights blinking red, then green, then yellow, then red, then green and yellow as she inched along. It's late for such heavy traffic, she thought. Then she remembered. It was almost Christmas. The Christmas shopping crowd would be keeping malls and streets packed for another week. She pulled into her apartment parking lot twelve hours after she left Atlanta.

Her things were still as she had left them, dusty but untouched. She wondered again about her parents. Hadn't they come over when she disappeared? What had they thought? What did they do? Did they call the police? Then she remembered the letter. She had written them a letter before she left, apologizing for her terrible transgression, for her shame, and telling them she had to go away to sort it all out. She'd explained that she would be out of touch for a while, and she didn't want anyone to look for her. They had obviously taken her at her word. When she saw them, what would she say? What would they say?

Meg collapsed on the sofa and stared at the name on the card. *Amy Roberts.* There was no way she could pretend to be someone else this time, something other than exactly who and what she was. What could she say to Amy?

Wait. Amy was her next task, the next person on her list of people to visit? Someone had told Nick that she needed help and wouldn't ask for it. That didn't sound like the woman Meg had known. She had always known Amy to be rich and spoiled, snobbish and condescending. What could have happened to her to make her worthy of their help? Maybe, just maybe, there was a little bit more to this story.

Exhausted, Meg decided to sleep first and tackle her task in the new day. She found that she felt less comfortable in this place that actually belonged to her than she had in any of the other strange places she had stayed. She lay down on top of the made bed and pulled the folded comforter over her like she was taking a nap. This time no dream lover came to wrap her in his warm embrace. She tossed and turned all night, unable to escape the ghosts of those she had wronged. Did she look different now that she was here? When she stepped out of her apartment would everyone she saw know that she was a wretched, miserable soul, as though she had a scarlet letter on her chest? She looked in the mirror and saw puffy eyes with dark circles staring back. Should she use the look for sympathy? Would people look at her and feel sorry for her torment? Did she deserve that compassion from anyone, even strangers?

Nick said it wasn't her crime, but she didn't believe him. He didn't understand.

She sat in her car, overwhelmed with the wrongs she had to put right. She had disappeared on her family without a word and abandoned her friends without explanation. She had humiliated Susan and destroyed her life, and she had caused the collapse of Richard Robert's publishing empire. She had run away and left them all to deal with the chaos she caused.

Amy Roberts. That was where she had to start. Stick to the job, and the job was finding out how to help Amy. What could have happened to her that caused her to be in need?

To start with, the address on Amy's card was different from the one that Meg knew was her boss's house. She found that it was an apartment building, nice and clean with beautifully landscaped grounds, but certainly not the mansion where she had been living when Megan had last seen her. She didn't have to even look for the apartment number, because she saw Amy sitting on a bench at the community playground, watching her children play on the colorful plastic play set.

She parked her car and squeezed the steering wheel to bolster her resolve. As she walked up the sidewalk and stepped onto the pine mulch she watched the emotions play across Amy's pretty face—first disinterest, then a smile of welcome, then recognition and surprise. She stood up but did not walk away as Meg had feared. "Megan," she said suspiciously, "what are you doing here?"

"I came to apologize, Amy, and beg your forgiveness, though I don't deserve it. I am so, so sorry for what I did." Her head hung with her shame.

"It was awful," Amy choked out as though she was going to cry, not angry as Meg had expected, but very, very sad.

"I know. It was a terrible thing to do."

"I knew, you know. I knew that he was sleeping with her. I was ignoring it to hold on to my nice life— big house, expensive cars and clothes, private schools for the kids. I couldn't face what I'd have to do if I left him, if he wasn't paying for everything."

Meg was flabbergasted. "But you got it. You got it all. The house, the clothes, the schools—he still had to pay. I know he did. I heard about the judgment before I left. When I saw him last I thought he was going to strangle me on the spot for what I had cost him."

"He may have wanted to strangle you, but you were just one on the list. He was angry with everyone but himself. He took me back to court and claimed I had cheated on him first."

"How could he do that? Surely he had to prove it?"

"He did prove it, because it was true." She sat down, and Megan sat beside her. One of the skills she had learned from her brief time with Nick was how to listen silently while someone else bared her soul.

Amy sat quietly for so long Meg wondered if she would talk at all, but at least she hadn't walked away. Finally she began in a voice so low she was almost talking to herself. "Jake had been coming over to the house for months while the children were in school. Richard had been abusive, of course, but only verbally. I had no police or medical records to provide as testimony because he never hit me. But that was no excuse. Cheating is cheating, and it is always wrong. I did it to have something to look forward to and to be with someone who paid me some attention, someone who made me feel sexy and desirable instead of like a block of concrete that held him underwater. It was exciting at first, you know, and I had that angry justification that he deserved it. Eventually I just felt dirty and low, like I had lowered myself to live in the muck. I cut off the affair, but not before Richard had gathered pictures and eyewitness accounts from the housekeepers to have in his arsenal against me."

"I'm so sorry."

"No reason for you to be sorry. You aren't the one who cheated on your husband. That night at the party? I wasn't hurt, I was humiliated. Our farce of a marriage was hung out there for everyone to see, but they all already knew anyway. They knew I was too greedy and shallow to leave a man who had no respect for me and ran around behind my back."

"It wasn't my place to hang it out, not that way, not at all."

"Maybe not. But you opened the wound and showed the horrible infection in it. It was puss-green and oozing, and it had to be stopped."

"Yuck." Meg made a face.

"Gross, but appropriate." Amy chuckled. "I would almost owe you a favor, if it hadn't been so horrible."

"What? Why?"

"Losing everything I thought I valued showed me what really mattered." She nodded at the playset. "A year ago I would have missed this. I would have been shopping or lunching with friends instead of watching my children play. Now we're together nearly all the time. They are my best friends."

Six-year-old Clint, five-year-old Jon and three-year-old Haley skidded to a halt in front of Amy, pushing the mulch into little piles at their feet. "Mom, we're hungry." Clint looked at Meg curiously.

"Yeah, Mom, is it lunch time yet?"

Amy looked at her watch. "I guess it is," she said, smiling. "Megan, will you have a bite with us?"

Meg fought the impulse to make excuses, certain that this warm welcome couldn't last. Even though she had been surprised by Amy's tale, she still didn't know why she needed help, and she couldn't leave until she had done her job. "Sure," she agreed, "thanks."

As they walked to the apartment, Amy held Haley's hand, but the boys ran ahead, the jangling keys ringing like bells with every step. Whatever curiosity they had about the stranger coming for lunch took second place to their eagerness to get home. Amy and Meg climbed the stairs and went through the open door to find the boys already sitting in front of the television turned to their favorite channel. Haley rushed to join them, dropping her jacket on the floor next to theirs as she went. A merry looking Christmas tree stood in the corner with a few small gifts peeking out from the low hanging branches.

Meg leaned against the counter as Amy went about the task of preparing sandwiches and soup. "Can I help?" she offered politely.

"No, thanks. Just stand here and talk to me. I don't get the chance to have real conversations with adults much."

"Do you mind my asking what happened? When I left you had the house and the car."

"I told you, he proved that I cheated first. His lawyer was better than mine, and he had been more deliberate in collecting evidence than I had been. The judge ruled that I had no right to alimony or the house or the business. I do get child support, at least for now." She let her hair fall down to hide her face.

"What is it? What's wrong?"

"He's taking me back to court. He's trying to prove I'm an unfit mother so he can take the children."

"What?" Even for a lowlife scum like Richard Roberts, this was unbelievably cruel. "Does he think he's more fit? Surely there's no way he can prove that."

"Actually, like I said, he has more evidence than I do. And he has a good job, a great job, with lots of money and lots of opportunities for the kids. My preschool teacher job is pitiful next to his. I can only offer them what he sees fit to give us."

"But surely everyone can see how they love you. There's no way the court will let him take them from their mother, especially while they're so small."

Though Amy's face was still hidden, her tears fell on the counter. "He doesn't care about the children. He only cares about being in control, about proving who has the real power. He'll pay a full time nanny or even send them to boarding school before he'll let them stay with me. He doesn't want to be with them. He wants to make sure that I can't. "

"I can't believe it." Meg had been so sure that Amy was a proud snob, that nothing could touch her charmed, affluent life, even if her husband was a cheating scumbag. If she had been that way once, she certainly wasn't any more. So this was how she needed help. She could not lose her children.

Surely Nick would know what to do.

Chapter 12

Meg left Amy and the children uncertain what to do and where to go. When the time was right, Nick had always appeared, but she had no idea how to contact him when she needed him, and he wasn't there. Every inch of her body felt electrified to move, to act, to do something, but she was unsure of what to do. She pulled into the parking lot of a strip mall, her thoughts overwhelming her senses so that she was too distracted to drive.

Why hadn't he come? What was he waiting for? Did she have something else to do before he got involved?

Of course she did. She had known all along that Amy was not the only reason she was here. She had to tie up her own loose ends. For better or for worse, she had to have closure to her past life before she could begin a new one.

Her first stop was her parents' house. On the long drive over she imagined a dozen different scenarios. Would they be so angry they'd tell her to leave? Would they be so hurt that she couldn't bear their pain? Would they berate her for the humiliation she had visited upon them with her behavior? She sat parked in the street outside her childhood home for a long while, steeling herself against their reactions. She hesitated at the door. A year ago she would have walked in without knocking or ringing the bell. Not today. The woman who grew up here no longer existed. She was a stranger, a mere visitor to this place.

Her mother opened the door. Like fast forwarding a movie, her face cycled rapidly through the full spectrum of emotions. The well-trained, polite welcome with which she always greeted visitors gave way to surprise. Surprise became shock. The shock caused her to sway unsteadily, causing Meg to grab her arm to keep her from falling. She expelled the breath she had been holding and tears overflowed her eyes to run down her cheeks. She pulled Meg into her arms and squeezed so tightly that Meg could hardly breathe. It didn't matter. She leaned on her mother's shoulder and cried like a little girl.

Her father came to see what was taking so long, froze in stunned silence, and then put his arms around both women, fighting the tears that men are never supposed to shed. They stood together, afraid to let go, afraid that outside their cocoon their reunion would disappear in a puff of smoke, the product of their collective dream.

Meg's mother guided her into the family room with a protective arm around her shoulder and sat with her close on the sofa. Her dad perched on the coffee table, elbows on knees, eager to have her story. "Where have you been?" he asked. "We called and called but you never answered."

"Hiding," she answered, "I've been hiding from my shame. I was too embarrassed to face even you."

"Oh, sweetheart." Her mom squeezed her shoulders. "You can always come home. We were afraid you were dead somewhere."

"I'm not going to lie to you, Megan," her dad said, sitting back, "we're not proud of your behavior. But what you did was not so wrong as what they had been doing. That Richard Roberts is a lowlife, cheating, son of a gun, and he deserved what he got."

"What he got was not much, as it turns out," Meg said.

"What do you mean?"

"I mean he's taken back everything his wife got in the settlement. She's living in an apartment and working in a preschool. Now he is trying to take the children, too."

"That's terrible," said her mom. "Surely he can't do that, can he, Tom?"

Her dad nodded. "It depends on his argument, but yes, if his lawyer is better than hers, he'll find a way."

"I don't want to talk about them. Tell me about you guys."

"Megan, where have you been? Why didn't you call us?"

Here it came. The guilt. She had known she would have to face it sooner or later. "I ran away, Mom, pure and simple. I couldn't face what I had done. I couldn't see them, all of them, any of them. What I did, I did in front of every person in the company, the ones who knew me and the ones who didn't. How could I see them every day? How could I see them at all? I couldn't, so I took the coward's way out."

"Where did you go?"

"I traveled around. No one place in particular." She was compounding her guilt with a lie, but the truth was too unbelievable to say out loud.

"Now you're back. Why? What has changed?" Her mother wasn't going to ask anything that might scare her away, but her father wanted to know more.

Meg sighed and took the question straight on, speaking the truth but leaving out the details. "I can't run forever, Dad. I have to take responsibility for what I did, put right what I can, and apologize for the rest. That's the way you raised me."

"Do you have a plan?"

"Sort of," She smiled. "Seeing you guys is the first step."

"Not the first if you've seen Amy Roberts."

She had to think fast. "I happened to run into her, believe it or not, before I could come and see you."

Satisfied that her daughter wasn't about to disappear into the ether again, Judy O'Riley slipped into mom-mode. "Have you eaten? Can I make you some tea?"

"I have eaten," Megan followed her into the kitchen. "but tea would be great."

"I'm going to call your brother." Her dad walked into his office. "He should come over tonight."

"Nobody 'should' do anything, Dad," Meg said, "I don't deserve it."

"Don't be ridiculous," he replied, "he'll want to see you. He's missed you, too."

Funny how the distance she had felt sitting in her car in the street had evaporated in her parents' loving embrace. She took the seat at the counter where she had sat hundreds of times in twenty-six years, from the first day she had to use the foot rest as a ladder to this day, her day of shame, her day of homecoming.

Her mom put the kettle on. Megan smiled and repeated her mother's words in her head as she said them. "Tea should never be made in a microwave. Waiting for the kettle to whistle is part of its healing power."

They both smiled as Megan repeated the last words with her mom.

"So what will you do now?" she asked.

"I have to see them," Meg replied. "I've seen Amy and made my peace with her, but I have to see Richard and Sue. I don't expect Richard to forgive me or even be sorry for his transgression, but I need to at least face him. I'll try to make peace with Sue. I don't expect us to be friends again, but she may at least accept my apology."

"Then what?" Judy asked, afraid of the answer.

Meg smiled and covered her mother's hand. "Don't worry, Mom. I won't disappear without warning again. That wasn't fair to you. Not fair at all."

"So you'll stay?"

"I honestly don't know. I've met someone, someone I like a lot, but I'm not sure what he wants."

"Really?" Her mother arched her eyebrows. "What's his name?"

"Nick," Meg answered, blushing.

The pink cheeks were not lost on her mom. "You're all flushed, dear. He must be pretty special."

"He is. He knows everything, and he helped me see that I had to come back. I have to mend the holes in my old life before I can move on to a new one."

"Can we meet him?"

"I don't know, Mom. Truly. He's not here with me, and I don't know if he's coming. He's like that, mercurial."

"Mercurial? Sweetheart, really? Must you make things even harder on yourself by taking up with someone you can't trust?"

"I trust him completely. He was so intent on my doing what I had to do that we never talked about what it meant for us. If there even is an *us*."

"Is he worth waiting for?"

"Most definitely."

"Well all right then. If he is telling you not to lose touch with us again, then I have to like him."

Her dad came back. "Mike's glad you're back, though I'm not sure he's going to be quite as forgiving

124

as we are. He's pretty upset with what you put your mother through."

"I know. Mom, I'm sorry."

"That's all right, darling, but please don't do it again."

"Right. But I do have to go for a bit. I have to go find Sue. I want to get that over and done."

Her dad was stern. "You don't owe her anything, Meg. That little tramp should have kept her hands out of another woman's cookie jar."

Meg sighed. "It's not that easy, Dad. Right or wrong, she trusted me. I owe her an apology for betraying her trust. That secret wasn't mine to tell."

"Fine," he replied, his voice flat. "Speak your piece then come home. No need for a long good-bye."

Meg smiled at the cliché. Her dad loved old movies and his speech was always sprinkled with a few famous lines. "Don't worry. I won't be long,"

Chapter 13

Meg caught Sue as she was walking out the front of their office building with everyone else leaving at 5 o'clock. A few people recognized her but were too stunned to speak. They found places to hide from having to converse with her themselves, but close enough to watch the show when she confronted Sue.

"You're leaving early," Meg said. Sue spun around. If she had been a cartoon, her eyes would have glowed red and bulged from her head. Instead, her glare made Meg take a step back out of the range of her grasp. "Hello, Sue."

Sue's chest heaved. Her mouth gaped open, but words wouldn't come. Finally she growled, "What are you doing here?"

"I came to see you. Can we talk somewhere? Please?"

"I'm not going anywhere with you," she spat. "Say what you have to say and go."

At least she was willing to listen. "I'm sorry, Sue. I want you to know how sorry I am. I'd take it all back if I could, even quit the job before it happened."

"It's a little too late for that, don't ya think?"

"Yes, but all I can do is say I'm sorry. What I did was unforgiveable, but I can't undo it."

"No, you can't." Icicles froze on her words, making Meg shiver.

Meg looked down at her feet, unsure what to do next. Should she walk away? Should she try to say more? Should she bait Sue to explode at her? Would it make her feel better if she got dressed down by this woman, gave her a chance to express all of her venom in one horrible bite? She thought part of her humiliation was Sue's icy silence forcing her to make the next move.

Instead, when she looked up she saw Sue's eyes filled with tears. "The worse thing was that I saw his true colors. I thought he loved me, thought as long as I said nothing I could keep pretending that one day he would leave her for me. I always knew deep down that it wouldn't happen, but I had the fantasy. You stole my fantasy, Meg. You grabbed it right out of my chest and threw it on the floor for everyone else to stomp on."

"I didn't mean to. I was upset about the way he was treating you. I couldn't stand for him to get away with everything he was getting away with. He was always scum."

"Yeah, you're the poster child for moral behavior."

"I guess so."

"So what now?"

"So nothing. I wanted to tell you how sorry I am and I hope that you'll forgive me someday."

"I accept your apology, but I can never forgive you for it." She paused, "And because of you, I can never forgive myself."

Meg started to walk away, then she remembered a question she had for her lost friend. "Why are you still here?"

"You mean why didn't he fire me?"

"Or why didn't you quit?"

Sue looked beyond Meg into the distance. "I make a lot of money here. Way more than you ever did."

Meg ignored the dig. She figured she deserved it.

"I wasn't going to give him the satisfaction of destroying my professional life as well as my personal life. It's been a year. I've stood my ground and made my point. Now I am looking for another job, and when it comes it won't look like I'm running away."

Meg nodded silently at Sue's solid reasoning. She wasn't some discarded entry level secretary who could move easily to another job any place that needed someone to answer the phones. She was an editor and a good one, one of the best. She had to wait for a position that matched up with her qualifications, a career move instead of a job. "I understand," she replied. "It was the right decision."

"I'm so happy you approve," she growled. "Good bye, Megan." She spun around and strode away.

Meg's legs were wet noodles. She leaned against the wall for support and willed her lungs to suck in air and push it out again. Where was Nick? He had always shown up when she needed him. Why hadn't he come?

She knew why. She had one more stop to make, one more bit of unfinished business. She pushed through the big glass doors to the reception desk, to find that Dave, the security guard for many years, still sat behind the counter. She saw that he sat alone, whereas always before there had been two guards, one to watch the desk at all times and one to handle situations. "Hi, Dave," she greeted him hesitantly. "Where's William?"

His eyes flickered recognition, but there was none of the friendly banter they had always shared. "He's gone," he replied, his voice leaving no doubt whom he blamed. "Can I help you with something?"

"Is Mr. Roberts in?"

"Just a moment, please." He pushed a button on the keyboard that made the intercom crackle to life. "A visitor for Mr. Roberts."

"Who is it?" Meg recognized the voice of Margaret, his long-time administrative assistant.

"Miss O'Riley."

Silence. Finally her voice came back tense and tight. "Send her up."

Dave nodded without speaking and turned his back on her. Conversation over.

When she had been working there the floor would have been busy and noisy well into the night, but whether because of the holidays, or because of the damage she had done, the silence was deafening. It was like a dream where everyone else in the world had vanished and she alone remained. "This way please," Margaret gave her an indulgent, professional greeting she would give a stranger.

Richard's pleasant demeanor chilled the air around them, the dark danger in his eyes a better warning of his mood than the forced smile on his face. He stepped around his desk and offered his hand. She hesitated, wondering if she should let him touch her. His grip was bone-crushing, and she thought for a moment that he would throw her through the window and send her plummeting fifteen stories to her death. She had to turn her eyes from his penetrating glare, feeling that he would to burn the skin off her skull, strangle her with his bare hands or slit her throat with the letter opener. "So you're back," he said with coolly controlled menace. "Good." He motioned for her to sit and moved back to his oversized leather throne. "Where have you been all this time?"

"Traveling," Meg responded. Her impulse was to bolt, but she had to finish her business first. "I came to apologize for what I did. I know it means next to nothing, but I wanted you to know that I realize the magnitude of what I've done and if I could take it back I would."

"I'm sure you are sorry, Megan," he responded, templing his fingers, "but that doesn't erase the transgression, does it?"

"No." She looked at her hands folded in her lap to escape his intense gaze. It didn't work. She could feel his eyes boring holes in the top of her skull like they were laser beams.

"Perhaps you should apologize to your former friend for betraying her trust."

"I have," she said in a small voice.

"And?"

"She cannot forgive me."

"And my children? Have you apologized to them for destroying their home and ripping their family apart?"

"No."

"Maybe you should. And the employees I had to lay off when I made budget cuts because of the financial strain you put on my business? Would you like a list of their names and contacts so that you can apologize to each of them?"

"I don't know." She didn't know whether to sob or scream. She needed to either die on the spot or get out, because she couldn't stand his remonstrations any more.

"You have apologized and I have acknowledged it. Is there anything else?"

"No, sir," she replied humbly.

"Well, then, thanks for stopping by. I believe you can show yourself out."

She was dismissed.

Chapter 14

Drained, Meg barely had the strength to drive to her parents' house. She would ask to stay with them instead of going to her own apartment. In all of her travels far from home, surrounded by strangers she had never felt as alone as she did at that moment.

Her brother's car sat parked in the driveway. She braced herself for the confrontation. Mike might understand and forgive her, but her sister-in-law would be a different story. Laura had never liked her. Even at their wedding, Laura had asked her grudgingly to be a bridesmaid and by and large had ignored her presence in favor of her own sister and friends. Megan had been isolated and completely out of place.

She didn't knock this time. Her parents still loved her. They still wanted to see her. They still wanted her to think of this house as home. Through the door she found that the quiet serenity she had found earlier in the day had given way to the energy of two very active grandsons. Their usual mania was amplified by the impending arrival of Santa Claus. They tackled her in the foyer as though she had never left.

"Megan, Megan," blurted seven-year-old Ryan. "There are packages for you under the tree. Big ones. Wanna see? Com'on. Com'on."

Simultaneously, calmer but louder to be heard over his little brother, nine-year-old Christopher tried to lay claim to her attention. "Grandma says Santa comes here, too. He did last year, do you remember? We got all those Legos, remember?"

Her brother came to her rescue. "Guys, give her a break. Let her get her coat off, for Pete's sake." He wrapped her in a warm embrace. "Welcome home."

"Thanks, Mike. I'm so sorry for everything I put you all through."

"Yeah, well, don't do it again."

Did he mean the dishonoring the family part or the disappearing part? "I won't." She meant it for either.

He led her into the living room where Laura sat sipping wine with her parents, and the boys had resumed their frantic examination of the beautifully wrapped packages under the tree. "Welcome home, Megan," she said through gritted teeth.

"Thanks, Laura," Meg replied meekly. Laura's insincere welcome was the reaction she had expected from everyone else.

Meg let the boys show her the packages under the tree with tags that read 'To Megan, Love, Mom and Dad.' She had only come home the day before, so how could there already be packages for her under the tree? She looked to her mother for explanation.

"We were hoping you'd be home for the holidays," she said, her eyes brimming with tears.

"Where are your gifts for us?" Ryan asked innocently.

"Hidden." Meg nodded. Presents. She had to get presents for everyone. How was she going to do that? Tomorrow was Christmas Eve. She had always been a good gift-giver, thoughtful and creative. It went against her nature to simply buy random useless trinkets just to have packages under the tree. Still, she had to do something. The adults would understand if she was late, but the kids would never forgive her, and she needed the good karma of kid-love.

She tried to focus on the warm, loving mood of her family gathering. After all, Christmas was still two days away, and this celebration was for her, the prodigal daughter returned. No matter how hard she tried, however, the meeting with Richard Roberts haunted her. Of all the scenarios she had visualized meeting Richard and facing his wrath, she had in no way anticipated the one that actually happened. His eyes were not flaming; they were ice cold. His voice was not shaking with emotion; it was hard and robotic. There had been no passion, no berating, none of the extremes of emotion she had prepared for. There was only that one statement hanging in between them. "So you're back. Good." That was it. That was his reaction to her. She expected that people would be enraged and tell her they never wanted to see her again. She never thought that one of those she injured most might have been eagerly awaiting her return. Why? Certainly not for anything good.

Lost in her thoughts, she was hardly aware of the doorbell until Mike ushered in another guest.

Nick.

He came straight to her, folded her into a loving embrace, and kissed her warmly, leaving no question in the minds of her stunned family as to the nature of their relationship. He kept one arm around her when he turned to meet her family. He knew, as he always knew, that she needed for him to hold her up.

He held out his hand to her father and mother then to Mike and Laura. "I'm Nick." He smiled. "I'm a friend of Megan's."

The boys ran up to him and pulled on his hand, "Com'on, Nick," they said as though they had known him all their lives.

"Guys, really?" Mike tried to stop them, embarrassed at their familiarity with a stranger.

"Don't worry, Mike." He spoke to the boys as though he had always known them. "I have to do adult stuff this time. We'll do fun things later, ok?"

"You promise?" asked Christopher.

"You have my word." Meg wondered why she had never noticed his accent before. His husky voice had always been soothing, but the British intonation was exotic and captivating.

Reassured, the boys ran back to the pile of Legos in front of the fireplace.

The adults returned to their seats. Nick's unexpected arrival had stirred things up, and their relaxed attitude had shifted to alert curiosity. Meg's mother sat on the edge of the sofa where Nick had settled in next to Meg, his arm protectively around her shoulders. "So Nick, how do you know our Megan?" She tried to sound casual.

"Funny to hear you call her 'your' Megan," he said, squeezing her shoulders, "I think of her as 'my' Megan. We met while she was in England."

Megan was stunned to hear the words come out of his mouth. She turned in his embrace to look at his face, but he just squeezed her again with a silent *I'm in control. Just go along with it.*

"You were in England?" Mike asked.

"For a while," Meg answered.

"And what do you do there?" Her mom did the talking while her dad watched suspiciously from his chair

Completely unaffected by their distrust, Nick smiled. "I am the director of a global charity," he replied. "Fortunately Megan could work with me there.

She has been particularly helpful in the last couple of months."

"Charity work, really?" asked Laura skeptically. She muttered under her breath, "Doing penance."

"Not at all," Nick said, looking directly at Laura. "Megan is incredibly kind. She has a way of seeing through to the truth of what people actually need."

He turned his attention on Meg as though she was the only person in the room. "Her services have been invaluable," he said intimately, "I hope she will continue to work with us in a permanent position after she has tended to her business here."

"Oh." Laura flushed.

"Not to worry, Laura," Nick didn't miss a single nuance of anyone's comments. "I believe I know a different woman from the one who left here last summer."

"Nick, will you stay for dinner?" asked Meg's mother.

"I would like that very much, thank you."

Meg was dying to talk to him privately, but didn't have her chance until after dinner.

"It has been a great pleasure being here," Nick said politely, "but I'm afraid I have to go. Megan, will you see me out?"

Nick's presence had lifted the stress and anxiety from every person in the house. The men shook his hand warmly, and the women embraced him, begging him to come back when he could. The boys launched themselves into his arms, and he caught them easily without missing a beat. "I owe you Lego time," he said, "I won't forget."

When he led Meg outside the familiar contentment radiated through her body from their clasped hands. "Walk with me," he said simply.

Since that first day in Cornwall, only by his side was she happy. When he wasn't there part of her was missing, though she sensed he was never far away.

"I'm so glad you came," she said, breaking the silence. "You completely charmed my family."

"They are easily impressed," he replied with a chuckle.

"Why did you do that?"

"Do what?"

"Talk to them that way. Act like we are in a relationship?"

"We are in a relationship, Meg," He paused. "Maybe we are not quite as well defined as I led them to believe, but it will ease their minds when you leave again if they know there is someone looking out for you."

"When I leave again?"

"Yes. Why? Were you planning to stay? Perhaps your intentions have changed since we last talked about them."

He was teasing. He knew her intentions had not changed, not unless he was so dense that he had missed the I-can-hardly-keep-my-hands-off-you and I-wish-you-would-stop-leaving-and-stay-with-me-forever messages in her body language.

He stopped them in front of a house lit foundation to roof with an explosion of Christmas lights. Each of the trees had been carefully wrapped in a different color, and the house itself was completely outlined in white. Tactfully designed wire reindeer, sprayed gold and covered with white lights, grazed delicately on snow covered grass. Large holly trees at each corner shone with strings of old-fashioned, large, colored bulbs. Far from gaudy or overdone, it looked magical.

Though she would not have believed it possible, Nick's face was even more handsome in the holiday lights. He leaned her against the fence and kissed her without hesitation, without remorse, without any inner conflict. She wrapped her arms around his neck, and he lifted her off the ground, pulling her up until she was eye level with him.

He let her slide down his body to her feet without loosening his embrace. "Please," she begged hoarsely, "please don't leave me again."

He pushed the hair out of her eyes. "I have to," he said, "I'm not done here and neither are you. We will take care of things, you and I, and then we can go home."

She closed her eyes and leaned heavily against him. "You know what happened today?"

"I do."

"What do you think?"

"I think you need to know there are a lot of people who love you. You have a dark time ahead before the sky clears, but when it does you will be rid of the heavy load you have been carrying."

"Will you be with me?"

"I cannot be there all of the time, but I will never be far away."

She closed her eyes and focused every bit of conscious thought on his good-bye kiss. When she opened her eyes he had vanished.

Chapter 15

Christmas Eve dawned bright and cold. Meg dressed early and had a quick cup of coffee with her mom before going out to buy gifts. She got in the car, checked the rear view mirror, and saw the back seat filled with presents she could not have found in any store. Richly colored sweaters for everyone draped the back seat. Music boxes for her mother and Laura sat beside a magnificently illustrated book on trains for her father, a railroad fanatic, and a throwback Washington Senators jersey for Mike, whose idol was Walter Johnson. The authentic Lionel train set for the boys made her grin. The old boys would love that toy, too.

When she pulled them out of the car she found one of the gifts already wrapped. Nick had left her a gift, too.

Wrapping the gifts began the fun for Meg, and for the first time in a long time she felt happy and excited. With her packages placed carefully under the tree, she spent the day helping her mom cook the endless list of family favorites for their traditional Christmas Day banquet. Through the caroling and the Christmas Eve church service, her anticipation grew. She felt like a little child. She even listened for reindeer hooves on the roof, believing as she hadn't for years that anything was possible.

Their Christmas Day began when Mike and Laura blew in with Ryan and Christopher, who couldn't wait to see what Santa had left at Grandma and Grandpa's house. The family stockings, one for each of them, that had been hung so carefully on the mantle since Thanksgiving, overflowed with candies, small toys, and luxurious adult sundries. Her mother, though a meticulous housekeeper, had made ashen foot prints on her perfect white carpet to enhance the illusion that a kindly old man in a jolly red suit had dropped down their chimney to leave gifts under the tree.

Her mom had not wanted to take anything away from the gifts Santa left for the boys at their house, so she had picked things to entertain them only when they visited Grandma and Grandpa. There were more Legos, of course, and a deluxe edition of Monopoly, a carom set and an *Avengers* checkerboard.

The boys assumed management of gift distribution. When each person had a stack of presents next to his or her seat, the wild rumpus began. Wrapping paper flew through the air and dropped like brightly colored snow. Everyone ooohed and aaahed over their gifts until only one gift remained. Nick's gift to Meg. She excused herself to the covered porch to open it alone. Though the boys in their frenzied state could barely stand to let a package out of their sight, the adults distracted them with the train set and Legos to give her privacy.

It was a first edition of *Winnie the Pooh*. Inside the cover Nick had written

Dear Meg,
Listen to the children. They have all the answers.
Love,
Nick

She hugged the book to her chest and longed for Nick's arms around her.

Chapter 16

December 26th arrived like a shade drawn to block out the sunny celebration of the previous days. The pain in her gut meant something bad was coming. At eleven o'clock it knocked on the door.

"Megan O'Riley, please?" asked the sheriff's deputy in full uniform, complete with his gun in its holster and his handcuffs in their pouch.

"I'm Megan O'Riley," she answered. Her parents easing up behind her.

"Megan Bridget O'Riley?"

"Yes."

"You are being served with a subpoena to appear in court on December 28th at 9AM." He handed her a business letter envelope and offered a clipboard to sign. He filled in the date and time and signed below her name.

"What is it?" asked her mother, guiding her gently inside.

"A subpoena," Meg answered. "Richard Roberts' attorneys are calling me as a witness in his custody trial."

"A witness for him? Why would they do that? Seems like what you know would hurt him more than help him."

"I would think so, but this means they have something up their sleeves. Something bad."

"I'm going to call Jimmy Rosen," her father said, reaching for the phone. "We need some guidance here."

Jimmy Rosen wouldn't get involved. Mike Tandoori wouldn't get involved. Joseph Levine wouldn't get involved. Finally Leonard White explained that Richard Roberts' lawyer, Buddy Dent, had a reputation for ruthlessly cutting down the competition. He was so skilled at eviscerating witnesses that he made the lawyers for the other side look like imbeciles. They all knew this case and they all knew that Amy Roberts had been through seven lawyers trying to hold on to her kids. The best any of them had been able to do was put off the decision.

"Amy didn't tell me that." Meg's blood was boiling. "Richard Roberts is a lowlife scumbag! I've felt so guilty for ruining his life, and he's taking it out on her."

"Meg, you didn't ruin his life. He should've kept his pants zipped," her father said.

"So I've been told."

"Told by whom?"

"Nick. Nick knows everything about what happened. He says I couldn't have told their secret if there wasn't a secret to tell."

Her father nodded. "Nick is a wise man. You should listen to him."

"Be that as it may, I still have to go to court, and I have no idea if there'll be any flesh left when the vultures are done tearing it off my bones."

Walking always helped Meg dissipate the fog in her brain. Where was Nick? He usually showed up at times like this. She willed him to be with her, even asked out loud, "Nick, please, I need you." She didn't expect it to work. He showed in his own time and for his own reasons. She looked hopefully at the face of every man she passed on the fashionable streets of

Georgetown, but to no avail. She did, however, recognize someone else.

"Megan." She heard a familiar voice call out from behind her. She turned to see the unbelievable truth. Dan Greene walked toward her.

"Dan, what are you doing here?"

"I could ask you the same thing."

"This is where my parents live," she said, processing through all the possible scenarios and conversations with the speed of a computer. "I'm home for the holidays."

"Boy, what a small world," he said, catching her in a warm embrace. "I'm really happy to see you."

"Thanks, you, too," she replied sincerely. She had truly enjoyed her time with him, feeling that they made a great team while they worked together. "What brings you up here? Your family's not from here are they?"

"Nope. One of my old professors from Georgetown is presenting a case to the Supreme Court, and he asked me to come and help him with a child custody case that isn't getting the proper attention."

"That's flattering, huh?"

"Sure is. Hey, I was looking for coffee. Do you have time for a quick cup?"

"As a matter of fact, I do."

Sitting by the window, Meg tried to sidetrack his inevitable questions by focusing the conversation on him. "So how are things going with the sister-in-law?"

Dan took a sip of his coffee. "'Bout as I expected. She is a very nice woman, and I enjoy talking to her. She knows a lot about the things I am interested in, so I can see why they keep trying to put us together. On paper we look like a great match, but there's no spark between us." He took a sip of his coffee and shook his head. "Truth is that's one of the reasons I'm here.

Debbie is pushing hard, and you saw how stubborn she can be. I had to get out of there."

Meg laughed. "She's Mighty Mouse. Here you are a great big guy letting this little woman push you around."

Dan grinned. "It's true. She's the irresistible force, but I am not an immovable object. So I took the coward's way out and got the heck out of Dodge for a few days."

When the conversation lagged, Meg braced herself. With the niceties covered, she was going to have to have a real conversation with this man who only knew her as a temp in Atlanta. Maybe he won't ask, she thought weakly. She should have known better. He was a lawyer. Interrogations were what he did for a living.

"So you're here for the holidays," he asked, "but you live in Atlanta?"

She thought about lying to him, but the truth was he might be the angel of mercy she needed. He was, after all, a lawyer, a dedicated lawyer. "No," she said, "actually, I live here."

"Then how did you come to be temping for me?" His question was obvious and justified, but she had no idea how to answer it. He watched her face intently, reading the emotions that played across it, though she tried hard to hide them.

Ultimately she decided to go with the truth about everything but Nick and his commission for her. That was so far beyond belief it would call everything else she said into question. "It's hard for me to say it, Dan, but here goes. I worked here as an editor, but I did something really stupid at a party that cost me my job. I couldn't face what I had done, so I took off, leaving everyone else to deal with my mess. I never even gave them a chance to fire me. I traveled around, taking temp jobs wherever I went. Working with you reminded me of how much I loved my job and my family, so I came home to mend fences."

"How's that working out?"

"Not so great. My ex-boss was so happy to see me that he served me with a subpoena," she said. "Merry Christmas, huh?"

"What you did, was it illegal?"

"No not illegal. Ill-advised, but not illegal."

"That's a tantalizing answer. Now you have to tell me."

She took a gulp of coffee, knowing that was all the stalling he'd accept. If she didn't answer he'd use his supernatural lawyer powers on her and break her like a witness on the stand. "I cornered my boss at a party and asked him when he was going to leave his wife for my best friend."

"Let me guess, the wife heard you."

"Yep, she was standing right there. Right there next to him, talking to my friend. The friend with whom he was having an affair."

"Ouch."

"You got that right. Brought down his publishing empire, more or less, at least I thought it did. He hates me, and needless to say, my friend, or rather my former friend, hates me. All of the other employees hate me for the chaos I caused with their jobs. I am the most popular girl at the ball," she said sarcastically.

"So why the subpoena?"

"Turns out I was wrong about a few things that I should have seen to before I left. I thought his wife had taken him to the cleaners, which he deserved, by the way, but that is not what happened. He hired better lawyers than hers. He hired private investigators who found out that she had been having an affair of her own. He kicked her out and cut her off and got away with a minimum amount of child support."

"That's lousy."

"You don't know the half of it. Now he is taking her back to court to take her children away from her. He's claiming she is an unfit mother. That's the case for which I've been subpoenaed."

"Why?"

"I have no idea, but I've seen him, and he is as cold and unforgiving as a steel girder. He's going to be ruthless in taking her down, and I play a part in that somehow."

"You don't know how?" Dan's friendly demeanor had shifted into lawyer mode.

"No, I don't. You would think I would hurt his case more than help it, since I can testify to his affair, but his lawyers have called me, not hers."

"You say it's a custody battle?"

"Yep."

"How old are the children?"

"Little. The two boys are barely old enough for school, maybe five or six, and the little girl is hardly more than a toddler."

"Do you consider her unfit?"

"No. I don't know her well, but I saw her with them a few days ago, and they are obviously happy and loved."

His jaw was set and the humorous sparkle in his eyes had been replaced with professional reflection. "So what could he possibly bring against her to claim she shouldn't have custody of them? You must know something."

"I don't. I hardly know her at all." He looked doubtful, so she added emphatically, "Really, I don't."

"He obviously thinks you do. Megan, this is the case I am working on. Richard Roberts vs. Amy Roberts. What an unbelievable coincidence."

"That is amazing," Meg agreed. Coincidence, Nick?

Dan continued, "It's actually lucky I ran into you. I probably even saw your name on the witness list and didn't put two-and-two together. He intends to blind side you and use something you've done or something you know to undermine her case. You need representation of your own. Someone to discover what they have in mind and prepare you for the questioning."

"We've tried. My parents have called all of their lawyer friends and friends of friends, but no one will touch it. Turns out we teased the wrong dog. Richard Roberts is well-connected and absolutely ruthless in getting his way. No one wants to look bad when his lawyers take them apart."

Dan sat back in his seat and squinted at Meg without speaking. She could see the gears in his mind turning, working through her problems, looking at the big picture and where she fit into his case. Finally he made his decision and leaned forward for emphasis. "Meg, it is questionable ethically for me to coach you, because you are supposed to be a witness for the other side, but the way they are behaving takes unethical to whole new level. In my experience it is pretty rare for a mother to be denied custody, and it is almost never good for the children. If you'll let me, I can help you prepare for your testimony to make sure he doesn't twist your words against her."

"Dan, I can't ask that. You hardly know me. Why would you do that for me?"

"A man tries to justify his own bad behavior by crucifying the mother of his children and hitting her at her weakest point. He's a schoolyard bully, and I'm the kid who's going to take him down."

"I'd appreciate the help, but it's still a lot to ask."

"You didn't ask, I offered. In fact, you could say I'm butting in uninvited." He grinned. "I love a good fight. Let me get a copy of that subpoena, and I'll see what I can do."

He walked her home, gleaning as many details as he could. She had known from her brief time with him that he was a lawyer prodigy, the youngest partner his firm had ever taken, and that he was absolutely obsessive over details, so that he rarely lost a case. It was an entirely different matter to have that attention turned on her, however, and she found herself wanting to do everything in her power to deserve his efforts.

When they walked into her parents' house, her mom and dad froze like statues, seeing that Megan had brought home yet another strange man. After an awkward pause, Meg explained the situation to them, and they recovered their manners. While Dan examined the subpoena with her father hovering over his shoulder, her mother pulled her into the kitchen. "Megan, dear, what did you do while you were gone?"

"I told you I traveled around, Mom."

"And you picked up strange men?" She was both shocked and disapproving.

"She worked for me, Mrs. O'Riley," Dan called from the family room, much to her embarrassment.

She didn't realize she was talking loud enough for him to hear her. She lowered her voice and asked, "Worked for him? You weren't even gone a year."

"I needed money, Mom, so I took some temporary jobs for living expenses." Her mother looked perplexed, and Meg knew she was thinking of the significant savings account she had sitting in the bank, more than enough to live on for months. "I didn't want to use my bank account because then everyone would know where I was." Meg put her hand on her mother's shoulder. "I had to have time, Mom, time to figure out what to do."

Dan and her father made a copy on the home printer, and then Dan was ready to leave. "This has the case number and court assignment," he said, "so I should be able to find out what I need from this. Your summons is for the day after tomorrow, so I've got to get busy. How about a ride?"

"Of course."

"Dan, this is awfully nice of you," Meg's mom said sincerely. "I don't know how we can ever repay you."

Dan flashed his *I'm-a-lawyer-in-control* smile and said, "Don't worry, my bill will more than take care of that." Then more seriously he said, "Meg helped me out when I was in a very tight spot, and she did great work. I'm happy to pay back that debt if I can."

Chapter 17

Meg was astonished when Dan asked to meet her at his professor's office at noon the next day. She showed up with the best pizza in Georgetown, to which Dan replied, "See? Feed me and I'll follow you anywhere."

Dan pushed aside the records regarding the Roberts' custody case that covered the table to make room for the pizza. Meg could see that they were covered with hand written notes and highlighted text. "I can't believe you've been over all this and so quickly. How did you do it?"

"Meg," he said, "in the one weekend you worked with me, didn't you notice how obsessive I am when I'm working on a case? Remember, I told you that I'm doing this to help out my professor. He wrote the book on Family Law. He had some of this stuff already, but all I have to do is drop his name and people give me anything else I want, particularly when I have them send it to his office here at Georgetown." He took a breath. "I told you, I don't like bullies."

"Richard Roberts is a bully, isn't he?" Meg agreed, glad to finally be talking to someone who understood.

"Worse than a bully. He is evil. See, look here." He pointed her attention to what looked like a conversation transcript. "This is her deposition. He hired private investigators to follow her around for a year before his affair came to light, so all the questions are based on their spy accounts and caught her totally off-guard. According to this interview, it appears to me that her affair began after his, after she had experienced neglect as a result of his attentions to this other woman. Her lawyers did not defend her against his charges, but let them stand without repudiation. They threw her under the bus to avoid a confrontation with him."

"He is a powerful man."

"No, he thinks he is a powerful man. There's a difference. He's convinced everybody else that he's great because he thinks he is, but he's not."

"Where do I come in?"

"His counsel expects to throw you off balance when they get you on the stand. They are planning to call your character into question to undermine your credibility in exposing him. Given your questionable, immoral behavior, would you not also find it easy to change the truth to suit your own ends? Secondly, they are going to ask you for concrete evidence of his affair. Did you ever see them together? Do you have anything to offer besides conversations with your friend? Are your actions the result of extreme jealousy of her relationship with a man you wanted for yourself? If you can't give actual eyewitness accounts, and even if you can, they'll try to have your testimony disallowed as unreliable and hearsay. All in all, they plan to make you look pretty bad. Your friend, too."

"Former friend."

"Right. Former friend."

"How do you know this? Their strategy isn't in the notes."

"I know people." He grinned. "Richard Roberts is not the only person with connections."

"That's great," Meg replied. "Now how can anything I have to say reflect poorly on her fitness as a mother?"

"His allegation is that she conducted her affair during times when she should have been caring for the children, and that she met with her lover at times when the children were with her. He's claiming that her lack of attention constitutes neglect and that meeting with this other man in their presence caused them harm. He's not denying his affair, but he is claiming that he never exposed the children to it, nor did he ever neglect his duties as a parent to make it happen."

"Duties as a parent? Don't make me laugh," she scoffed. "He didn't compromise his duties as a parent because he didn't have any. She had full responsibility for them 24/7." She paused. "You know, at the time I thought she was rich and spoiled, but that was because I only had his side of the story. After talking to her and seeing her with the kids, there's no doubt in my mind that she is their go-to person for everything they need. They adore her. It breaks my heart to think she might lose them."

"I understand that, but emotion cannot come into this at all, otherwise we can't get the job done. We have to prepare you for your examination so you don't come off as an immoral provocateur."

"Dan," she asked humbly, "how do you know I'm not an immoral provocateur? You hardly know me, and you weren't there to see what I did."

He put his hand over hers. "Meg, I am an excellent judge of character. Your shame over this incident, which is unwarranted, by the way, tells me all I need to know about the person you are. Your self-imposed guilty sentence needs to be repealed. An error in judgment, perhaps, but that is not a crime."

A tear slid down Meg's cheek and fell on their clasped hands.

"Don't worry," he said, "I'll get you through this."

Chapter 18

Meg wanted to laugh out loud at the surprise in Richard Roberts' lawyers' eyes when Amy arrived in court with Dan's professor, Joel Woodhouse, at her side. Dan had explained to her that he was a legend in Family Law because most practicing lawyers had used his text book in law school. They had sent the files, so they knew that he was her attorney, but they obviously hadn't expected him to show up with her himself. They didn't know that Dan had done all the footwork, but Dr. Woodhouse was more than willing to make time in his schedule, because he, too, hated bullies, but more than that, he knew Richard Roberts and wanted to reveal him as the lowlife he was. He took the case for that reason in the first place.

They had planned to discredit Megan, but, thanks to Dan, they couldn't. He had helped her remember little occurrences that gave evidence of her genuine knowledge of the affair, gifts she had seen, flowers he had sent, and phone calls she had overheard. She was able to turn their questioning of her moral character because of her bad behavior at the party into a sympathetic, if misguided, effort to advocate for her friend. They might prove Amy was an unfit mother, but not with her help.

On their way out Joel Woodhouse led Amy to speak to Meg and Dan. "Dan," Joel introduced him, "this is Amy Roberts. Amy, this is my friend and former law student Dan Greene. He's helping us with your case."

Meg had forgotten Dan had never met Amy. His job-well-done attitude dropped like he had been hit by a lightning bolt. He took Amy's hand in both of his. "Mrs. Roberts," he said, "it's nice to meet you."

Tears welled in Amy's eyes. The warm handshake and kind words penetrated her proud façade. In one brief visit, Meg had come to like and admire Amy and discovered quickly that she deserved any help Nick could give her. But here, in the cold halls of the courts with their marble pillars and soaring ceilings, she looked like a lost child. Meg put her arm around her shoulders and read the expression on Dan's face. He was ready for a fight.

"Com'on," Dan said, "I'm treating lunch."

"I've got to go," Joel said, his body already angled toward the door. "I'll leave them in your capable hands."

Lunch was full of pleasant conversation and general camaraderie, with an unspoken understanding to take a reprieve from legal talk. Funny, Meg thought, how someone as slimy as Richard can make fast friends out of his enemies. After the bill came, when it was time for Amy to meet Joel back at the courthouse, she spoke in a soft voice. "Thank you. Thank you both. At least you are one person he couldn't use against me."

"Amy," Meg asked, "what's going to happen? How are you going to fight this?"

"I don't know," she replied sadly. "Richard is holding all the cards. When we first started these custody discussions the lawyers said I had nothing to worry about. Courts always favor the mother, they said. That was before they realized who I was dealing with. Joel is doing his best, but there's just no time." Her tears flowed freely and her breath caught in her chest. "He's going to take my babies. He's going to take my babies, and he doesn't even want them." Her sobs made speaking very difficult. "He's doesn't…care …about them…at all. He just…wants to…to punish me…in the worst…the worst way possible."

Dan and Meg exchanged glances. "I can help you," Dan said, "That's why Joel has me up here."

"Really? You think there is something you can do?" Amy pleaded.

Dan winked confidently at Meg. "After court today I'll consult with him," he said, "and I'll get back to you tonight. He knows I don't like bullies. This guy is going down."

Dan was ebullient when he jumped out of Meg's car at the university. His computer-like mind had been processing the problem constantly since they left Amy, and determination, enthusiasm, and moral outrage shot out of his body like fireworks.

"What about the other work you are doing for Dr. Woodhouse?" she asked. "Remember, the Supreme Court?"

"Yep," he replied breathlessly, "if I'm going to do both I need more coffee. Lots and lots of black coffee."

"Dan…" Meg started, embarrassed for what she had gotten him into.

"Meg," He forced himself to slow down and emphasize each word, "Amy had an affair, yes, but in that her crime is no worse than his. Based on my own observations and what you have told me, it is obvious those children belong with her. They are the innocent ones here, and I won't let this guy ruin their lives because his counsel is better at manipulating the law. It cannot be tolerated."

"Thank you," she said, humbled in the light of his passion.

"Absolutely." He grinned. "See you tonight."

Chapter 19

When Dan got in the car that evening, he had an accordion file overflowing with paper. "My goodness," Meg said, "what have you done?"

"Not so much as you think," he replied. "Their case is pretty weak."

"Still, that's a lot of work."

"Not to worry. Joel agrees that this is important, and he knows I'll stay up all night as many nights as it takes to get this done."

"What about sleep?"

"Sleep is for old ladies and wimps."

"I like to sleep. Most people do."

"I'll have plenty of time for that when I'm old."

Meg knew he wasn't posturing. She'd seen him go at it the weekend she worked with him.

She drove him to Amy's apartment and walked him up. When she opened the door, a wonderful aroma wafted out.

"Boy, it smells great," Dan said, removing his coat and helping Meg with hers.

"It's just chicken and rice," Amy replied shyly, "I didn't know if you would eat before you came."

"I didn't," he replied. "Chicken and rice sounds great."

Meg saw three little faces peeking out of the hall. She touched Dan and nodded toward them like she was trying to keep skittish rabbits from hopping away. Amy smiled.

"So," said Dan loudly, "you said you had children, but this place is far too quiet for there to be children here. Do you have them locked in cages with muzzles like dogs?"

"We're not locked up," said Clint, stepping into sight with Jon and Haley hiding behind him. "We're not even quiet."

"Oh," said Dan, "I see. Well it seems pretty quiet to me."

"Mom said this was an important meeting and we needed to be good." Clint replied matter-of-factly. "I'm making the others behave."

"Thank you…" He looked to Amy for a name.

"Clint," she replied.

"Thank you, Clint. And who is hiding behind you?"

"This is Jon. And that's Haley. She's just a baby."

"I'm not a baby," Haley protested, stomping her foot.

Dan was enchanted. "Amy, it is obvious that these children are unsupervised and unloved. How dare you try to keep them!" Then, low enough that only Amy and Meg could hear, he said, "Don't worry. There's no way I'm letting that son-of-a-gun take them away from you."

As minutes stretched into one hour then two, Haley interrupted them by poking her mother's leg, her blanket lovingly clutched against her chest, her thumb in her mouth. "Mama," she said in a little tired voice, "I want to go to bed."

Dan shifted his attention to the three-year-old. "Haley," he said kindly, without condescension, "We're almost done here. Give me a few more minutes with your mama, and then I'll leave and she's all yours. Okay?" The little girl nodded, but still looked like she was going to cry. "Would you like to sit up here and see what we are doing?" he asked, scooping her up into his lap as Meg had seen him do with his niece.

Haley looked with interest at the papers on the table for a couple of minutes, and then she leaned back, cradled in Dan's left arm. She battled her heavy eyelids for a few minutes until her head dropped against his chest. They worked another half an hour until Dan closed the files and rubbed his eyes with his free hand. Amy lifted the limp child off his lap. "Man, it's cold now." He grinned. "She's a great little heater." Shifting rapidly into his more serious persona, he said, "I'll have everything ready for Joel to represent you." He and Meg shrugged into their coats. "First thing we have to do is get that court date moved up so we can finish this before I have to go back to Atlanta. I'll take care of that tomorrow."

Amy kissed him on the cheek. "Thank you," she said, her voice throaty with emotion.

Meg dropped Dan off at the university library where he planned to spend the night working. She felt guilty and said so.

"Not to worry," Dan replied energetically, "I'm good with this."

When she pulled into her parents' driveway, she saw the shadow of a familiar figure rocking on the garden swing. She sat next to him, matching the rhythm of his to-and-fro.

"You planned this whole thing, didn't you?" she asked.

"A good chemist can hypothesize the outcome of mixing reactants," he replied. "It doesn't always work out, but I can get pretty close with an educated guess."

"You did better than that." She looked at him slyly.

"It's true that the way these dominoes were set up, they seemed likely to fall this way. But we started this project many months ago. You are the catalyst that set the reaction in motion."

"So is this a chemistry metaphor or a domino metaphor?"

"They both work, don't they?" Nick smiled. "Either way, what needed to happen is happening." He smiled his mysterious smile and put his arm around her. "No more questions, Megan. It's time to go home."

Like a video she played back the events of the last weeks, the people she had met, and the places she had been. She had the sense that she was floating, a nebulous consciousness separated from the hard solidness of reality. *I never really belonged here.*

"No, you didn't," Nick read her mind and responded aloud.

"I am not this person. That is why I never fit."

"That's right."

"You knew. You knew and you had to show me where I belonged."

"Yes."

"I'm ready."

"You must see to your family first. *Primum non nocere.*"

"*Primum non nocere?*"

"First, do no harm. You must settle things with your parents so they are not hurt by your leaving. I will come back for you on the new year."

"Will I see them again?"

He pulled her to her feet and into his embrace. "Yes. It is not *adieu* 'Go with God.' It is *au revoir* 'Until We Meet Again.' Besides I owe the boys some Lego time."

Chapter 20

In addition to all the other lessons she had learned in the previous few weeks, Meg had finally discovered the most important truth of all. Guilt is a very selfish emotion. It focuses all of a person's energies inward and obscures the good she could be doing if she simply apologized for her mistakes and moved on.

Freed of her horrible burden and knowing that her time was limited, she focused all of her attention outward on those around her. She listened to them talk and actually heard what they were saying. The last few days she had with her family were more illuminating than the entire lifetime that had come before.

She discovered that her mother was depressed to be aging and worried about being less attractive to her father. This concern was exacerbated by her father's increasing self-absorption. When Meg paid close attention to her father's behavior, she realized he often had a blank stare when he was addressed. One tiny experiment, speaking behind him then saying the same thing to his face, solved the mystery. "Have his hearing checked," she told her mom. "He's not less interested in you. He can't hear you."

She wondered how at Christmas she had missed the tension between her brother and his wife. When they came in the next night, Meg noticed that Mike left Laura at the door and quickly took a place on the sofa to watch football with their dad. How many times over the years had they come in and Meg had failed to see the unhappiness and hurt on Laura's face? Perhaps her sister-in-law's coldness and condescension was a mask for something much more personal. Meg and her mom had often spoken unkindly about Laura behind her back. It was time to see what she had to say face-to-face. "Come have a cup of coffee with us," Meg asked her cheerily, rescuing her from the incessant onslaught of men and sports. They hadn't been nursing their cups long before Laura unburdened her heart. Mike had no respect for her because she didn't work for money. Even though they had decided together that she should stay home with the boys fulltime, he took no interest at all in the events of her days.

Her mom put a comforting hand on Laura's arm, and for the very first time spoke to her like a mother. "Don't let him get away with that. You have a right to that respect. Stand your ground and make him listen. It may take a time or two to train him, but he will learn that you are a force to be reckoned with." She chuckled. "He's my son, and I love him more than life itself, but he is still a man."

Meg left her mother and sister-in-law to married woman talk and went in search of her nephews. She found them in the living room, building an extravagant city of Legos. "May I help?" she asked. She sat next to a pile of blocks and started to assemble a complex, awe-inspiring, Frank Lloyd Wright example of Lego structural design when a thought wedged itself in between her glorious ideas. "What do you guys need?" she asked, taking a look at the elaborate model in front of her. Like cleaning a dirty window, she suddenly saw it through their eyes. There was obviously a plan that her adult eyes couldn't make out, and she needed to let them to explain it.

"We need a zoo," replied Christopher without looking up from his project.

So she made a zoo that matched the existing architecture.

A quick call to Dan revealed that he had indeed been able to move the court date to the next day. Thanks to the prestige of his professor, the judge would hear their case over his lunch break.

Showing up at the hearing to lend moral support, Meg's heart warmed to see Dan and Amy holding hands and Richard Roberts not happy about it. The self-satisfied smirk he usually projected had morphed into his true demonic visage, a heartbeat away from horns and a pitchfork. He was no longer in control of the situation and could not guarantee its outcome. Joel Woodhouse was so skilled an attorney, and Dan had prepared him so well, that the judge still had time for lunch when they were done. In fact, he made Richard and his legal team look like idiots for even trying. With quick hugs and thanks, Meg watched Dan and Amy walk away hand in hand, and she felt happy.

Their family New Year's Eve tradition was a party at the Thompson's house, their neighbors for twenty-five years. It was an elaborate shindig of fifty of their closest friends and children, with a bountiful pot luck table and free-flowing liquor. Meg stood alone enjoying watching the children playing with sparklers. When familiar arms encircled her from behind her heart swelled.

"Happy New Year," Nick whispered in her ear.

She turned and wrapped her arms around his neck, pulling him down into a kiss. "Happy New Year to you, too."

Mike walked up, his eyes widening in surprise when he saw Nick. His shocked expression was immediately replaced with enthusiasm, and he took

Nick's offered hand with a firm grip. "Great to see you, man," he said. "When did you get back in town?"

"Today," Nick replied without missing a beat, "I wanted to start the New Year with your sister."

Mike grinned. "I know she's glad to see you. In fact, I can see her blushing in the dark."

Embarrassed, Meg looked away, but Nick tightened his embrace.

Chapter 21

Leaving was much easier than Meg had expected it to be.

"It is so soon for you to leave," her mom choked out, tears brimming in her eyes. "Can't you stay a bit longer?"

"I love you, Mom, you and Dad so much." Her heart filled to overflowing, she held on tight to her mother, hoping she could feel it rising in her chest. "But I have finally found a place where I belong. Funny thing is I didn't even know I was looking until there it was."

"I don't suppose Nick has anything to do with it?" she teased, easing the sadness that threatened to overcome them both.

Meg grinned and blushed, as though she had tried to keep secret what everyone saw clearly from the moment they met him. "Maybe. A little."

"I'm so very glad, sweetheart. He is a good man, and he loves you. It is all over his face." She hugged her daughter tightly again. "I don't know why he ever leaves when it is so obvious that he wants to be with you."

Meg smiled and looked to where Nick talked with her father. He caught her eyes and winked. "He's a busy man, Mom, but he has promised me he will always come back, and I believe him."

"I believe him, too," she said as they moved, arms around waists, to where the men were standing.

Her dad grabbed her in a desperate hug. "Nick has promised he'll take good care of you," he said, "and that he'll see you make it home every now and then."

"I will. You have my word," Nick confirmed, reaching for Meg's hand. "We'll call to let you know when we are safely home."

Meg squeezed his hand and thought how far she had come in only two months, from having no home to having two. One was the home of her past. The other was the home of her future.

Whatever magic or sorcery Nick used to travel, he did not use it for this trip. She drove the whole long way back to the Smoky Mountains, to the secluded place where she could hide her car. Nick, as usual, had very little to say, but the silence was comforting, not uncomfortable, and she left the radio off to enjoy it. They hiked to the carefully camouflaged cave. Snow waited inside, prancing and pawing impatiently at the dirt floor, anxious to be off on their journey. She nuzzled Nick in greeting, and then nudged Meg with her velvet nose and a puff of warm breath.

Before they climbed onto the horse Nick turned her in his arms to face him. "Thank you," he said sincerely. "Thank you for all that you did."

She looked at him coyly. "I didn't think I had a choice."

He spoke not a word but tightened his embrace and leaned down to kiss her, a long, slow, breathtaking kiss. He mounted and reached down to help her climb up behind him.

Going back was far less stressful than leaving had been. She wrapped her arms around Nick's waist and rested against his strong, solid back. Snow's pace was steady, not frantic as before. Meg closed her eyes and expelled all the anxiety of the last two weeks with slow, deep breaths.

They arrived in the village to find a celebration in full swing. In the night, millions of twinkle lights filled every tree and lined every window. Bonfires had been built all around the party site, creating a bubble of warmth for the revelers. Hoots, hellos and hurrahs cheered their arrival, with handshakes and hugs all around. Bobby grabbed Nick's hand and pulled him to where a crowd of children built an elaborate snow fort. Molly wrapped Meg in loving, big-sister arms and told her that her room was just as she had left it, waiting for her return.

"What are we celebrating?" Meg asked, taking in the long tables filled with food, the extra bright lights on the bandstand, the boisterous Celtic music and ebullient dancers.

"Christmas. New Year's. The winter solstice. Anything and everything," Molly replied cheerfully. "Come and dance." She grabbed Meg's hand and pulled her into the circle of gleeful dancers, twirling and skipping and gliding, moving in and out and around to the beat of the drum, the pump of the accordion and the stroke of the fiddle's bow.

When the flautist lowered her instrument to sing a lyrical ballad in a soft, soothing voice, Meg found Nick once again at her side, pulling her into his arms for a sweet, slow dance.

"So you dance?" she teased. "Another secret of the mysterious Nick revealed."

"It has to be the right girl and the right song," he responded, seductively running his fingertips up and down her back.

He pulled their clasped hands to be pressed between their bodies, and they swayed quietly to the melody until the interlude was over and the wild rumpus began again. Nick led her away from the chaos and out from the town to the beautifully hushed, snow-covered fields.

"Something is different," she said quietly so as not to disturb the peaceful scene.

"Yes," he replied simply.

"Tell me," she said, leaning forward to see his face as they walked.

"We have accomplished our goals for this year," he replied. "Now is the time for other things."

"Like what?" she asked, hoping she was reading his signals right.

He did not reply but led her back to the old Victorian. Its panoramic view now included the lights and music of the festivities in full swing below. Unlike the last time, it was not brightly lit from every door and window, but instead gave off a soft glow as though filled with candlelight. Inside she found that, in fact, there were lit candles and lanterns strewn casually throughout the house. As before, a welcoming fire popped and crackled in the fireplace, but this time the only other light came from the Christmas tree in the corner, completely decorated from base to crown.

When she was seated on the sofa, he retrieved a stack of papers from his cluttered desk and deposited them on the coffee table in front of her.

"What is this?" she asked.

"Look at these letters," he began. "What do you notice about them?"

"They are all written by children," she said thoughtfully, "and they are all addressed to Santa Claus. Are you Santa Claus?" she asked, joking, sort of. "That would explain a lot."

"Children write millions of letters to Santa every year," he said, ignoring the question, "and the requests in most of those letters will be taken care of by their parents. Charities often fill the need if parents can't. Some letters, however, stand out because they ask for gifts for adults in their lives. Those requests are usually ignored. Adults don't play Santa Claus for other adults."

"I don't understand."

"You see," he explained, "children are naturally self-centered. They have to be. It is a holdover from a time when their entire focus had to be on survival, and they were completely dependent on demanding what they needed from those who could provide for them."

"Not all children are selfish," she replied thoughtfully.

"I didn't say selfish. I said *self-centered.* There is a difference in terms of attitude. Selfish people feel they are entitled to anything they want, regardless of the needs of others. Self-centered people merely have no other obligations and so see everything relative to their own needs and experiences. When given someone else to focus on, self-centered people will often step up to do what they can."

"Fair enough."

"If a letter from a child pleads for a gift for someone else, it usually means there is something going on significant enough to draw his or her attention outward. These are the letters that sent you on your journey."

Dear Santa, Please bring Mama money, said the first from Ophelia's Max, *she works real hard and we're tired of eating spaghetti all the time.*

She didn't know the next child, but there was no question about whom she was writing. *Dear Santa,*

Please bring my grandma Ohio paints. Her Tennessee paints won't work here.

The effusive energy of Dan's nephew, Ethan, came through the obviously dictated words on his page. *Uncle Dan needs Star Wars light blasters to play with me. He won't play without them.*

Clint's letter moved her deeply, but she was satisfied to know his need had been relieved. *Dear Santa, Please bring us a new daddy,* he wrote in his childish scrawl. *Ours is really mean.*

The last one broke her heart. It was from Eddie's Suzanne, who wasn't as okay as he and Natalie had thought. *Dear Santa,* it said. *I want to go home. Eddie and Natalie need a mom and dad, too.*

"I know how you solved Dan and Amy's problems," Meg said. "That was pretty smart. Dan needed to have more life than work, and Amy needed a decent man in her life. They were each other's gifts."

"Not exactly," he replied. "No one can control the human heart or make someone feel something they wouldn't have felt anyway. In that case we were just planning on Dan helping Amy with her case. Their falling in love was an unexpected bonus. "

"So explain these things to me," she said, still uncertain.

"Easy enough, really," replied Nick. "Ophelia needed money, yes, and urgently. We put an envelope under her landlord's door with enough money to cover her rent, and we paid off her lay-away so her children could have Christmas, augmented, of course, by a few toys handmade by our own *elves.* We also dropped an anonymous gift into her bank account to keep her afloat for a little while."

"That's a lot of money."

"Yes, we make a lot of things to sell throughout the year, and our income is substantial. It is all to help out in situations just like this one. But what Ophelia really needed was a more permanent solution. That is what she found under her tree."

"How?"

"She discovered a mysterious gift from a secret Santa. It contained a laptop computer and a college catalog highlighting the director of the nursing school who just happens to be Rosalie McGinnis. Remember the man Ophelia calmed the day you were there? That is her father. She recognizes Ophelia for the angel on earth that she is. She is eager to help her father's caregiver in any way she can." He rolled his eyes in feigned innocence. "We may also be the anonymous donor that set up a scholarship for her. Just to make sure they put all the pieces together."

"Nursing school, huh? Very clever."

"We thought so," he said with a grin. "'Give a man a fish, and he eats for a day...'" He trailed off so Meg would finish his sentence.

"'Teach a man to fish, and he eats for a lifetime.'"

"That's right. Ophelia doesn't need a handout, she needs a better job. See how it works?"

"You're good," Meg said. "Tell me more. Lyda needs Ohio paints? How are they different from Tennessee paints?"

"We took those Ohio paints and dropped them at her granddaughter's school, which no longer has a budget for an art teacher. Imagine their relief to discover that a new art teacher has moved to town, and she is willing to work for free. Lyda does need to be near her children, but she doesn't have to be dependent on them. She needs a life of her own and a new reason to carry on." He paused. "And believe it or not, they don't realize they are doing themselves a favor, too. It can be helpful to have an extra pair of hands and an extra driver when you are working parents with young children. All together, that is a win-win situation for everyone."

"Very clever. What about Eddie? Eddie and the girls don't need clever. They need parents."

"Yes, they do." Nick nodded. "And there's one waiting for them."

"What?"

"They've been gone two years. A few things have changed that they don't know."

"What do you mean?"

"Their mother's sister was just starting her career when their parents died. At the time she didn't think she could care for three children. She never meant to abandon them, however, and since the moment they ran away she's been looking for them, determined to make a home for them, no matter what."

"Are you going to tell her where they are?"

"She already knows. She went to Florida last week and stayed at the resort where Eddie works."

"Did they recognize each other?"

"They did."

"So they had a home by Christmas, just as you promised. Well done," Megan said. "That's Ophelia, Lyda, and Eddie. I'm assuming you solved Dan's problem with Amy, like you solved Amy's problem with Dan."

"It's a little more complicated than that. In fact, as our usual projects go, this one was very difficult to put in place," Nick said with a heavy sigh.

"What do you mean?"

"This is a long one. It's your story, as well."

171

Meg was pensive. Was she ready? She decided that she was. "I'm ready," she said leaning back against the cushions.

Nick leaned on the mantle and stared into the fire. "The first letter we got this year was from Amy's children. They visited a Christmas shop near Baltimore that has a Santa Letter Box for children year round." His voice cracked and he cleared his throat. "Most children are afraid of getting in trouble close to Christmas, and so their letters make them look like perfect angels. Not this one. You could feel the pain coming off the page. This child's father was making his little life very, very hard."

He looked at her. "I sent another agent to evaluate that situation earlier in the year the same way that I sent you. He was a guard at the front desk. Remember? You noticed he was gone when you went back.

"He discovered that Richard Roberts is a human black hole. People wander randomly into his orbit, and he absorbs every bit of light and life they have. When he is done with them, they barely exist at all. There is only empty space where a person used to be. All of this time you were feeling guilty for what you had done, it was your actions that brought together the elements necessary to resurrect his victims. What you did actually freed Amy and Susan and yourself, for that matter, from his gravitational pull, but it didn't repair the damage he had done and was continuing to do. We needed a positive force strong enough to overcome his negative one. After your report on Dan, I knew we had found the person we needed."

"So the different stories didn't start out intertwined?"

"Not at all."

"And what I did wasn't bad?"

He smiled. "I wouldn't generally recommend it. You did show a significant lack of judgment, but it certainly wasn't necessary to torture yourself. For you it was an embarrassment, nothing more. And as I said, sometimes a bad thing can be turned to good use."

"So Dan was the key?"

"Dan is a person of uncommon integrity and compassion and a forceful legal talent. It also doesn't hurt that he is physically imposing. All of those qualities make him an avenging angel to battle Richard Roberts' sadistic devil. We just had to bring all the pieces together."

"So my role in all of this was bringing them together."

"It didn't start out that way. We didn't know what they would need or how we could help them until you got in there and showed us. That was when we could see how our gifts could best be used. All we had to do was send Dan an autographed copy of his professor's book, cleverly disguised as one of those funny, unexplained packages under the tree that no one can remember putting there. He called him that night to congratulate him on his success, and that's when Joel Woodhouse explained that he had too much work on his plate and asked him to come up for a few days to help."

He sat next to her on the sofa. "You were one of the victims, you know, but by the time we discovered from William how many people actually needed our help you had disappeared. It took a bit of doing to find you."

"You looked for me? But I thought you only helped people from children's letters."

He pulled another letter out of his pocket. She recognized Ryan's childish scrawl. *Bring Aunt Megan home for Christmas*, it said, *she is the gift we want most of all*. It was more than she could stand. She covered her face with her hands and cried.

Nick pulled her hands away from her face and smoothed her tears with his thumb. "We already knew about Richard Roberts and how many lives he had destroyed. Imagine my surprise when another of his victims turned up at my doorstep. I watched you myself from a distance once you got to Cornwall. It was obvious that you had reached a point of utter despair."

"So you brought me here?"

"Yes."

"That was my gift?"

"Yes. Your solution could not be left under a Christmas tree or in a stocking on the mantle. You needed to discover your true value."

"So like Ophelia and Lyda, you have given me meaningful employment."

He smiled. "Yes."

"Is this a job I can keep?" she asked hopefully.

"If you want to," he replied.

"I do."

"You must be certain. It means leaving home and family. It means not seeing them for long periods of time."

"I can't see them at all?" The words that stuck in her throat were hard to choke out. Her family. She just got them back, and they just got her back. Could she do that to them again?

"Of course you can. I wouldn't make a promise to your parents that I didn't intend to keep. And do you think I could deny those little boys their aunt? The aunt who was their Christmas present? I promised them I'd come and play Legos. I have to do that before they get too old to care."

"This is like no place I have ever been," she said hesitantly, "and I have known happiness here I never dreamed existed for me anywhere." She swallowed her fear and summoned the courage. "Nick, I like this job. I like it a lot. But its greatest appeal is staying with you. What I want more than anything else is to stay with you."

Her revelation did not cause the happy surrender she had hoped. "There is more you need to know before you make that decision," he said solemnly.

Here it came, the hope crusher she had been expecting. "What do I need to know?" He stood and held out his hand. They were leaving again. Where were they going this time?

"Come," he said.

Chapter 22

They were going farther than she thought. He led her through town to the stables where Snow waited. All the other horses slept, but she knew. She was ready.

Nick climbed on the great beast behind her this time. They entered the tunnel at such a leisurely pace that Meg wondered how they could ever get where they were going before she was old and gray. When Nick leaned back in the saddle and pulled her against him, her curiosity slipped into a languid desire that they would never arrive. In the utter blackness, without any input at all from her eyes, she became keenly aware of every point, line and plane where they touched. His embrace yielded no space for her to squirm away, as if she would have even if she could. Their bodies swayed as one on the back of the big horse. She surrendered her personal space and allowed him to occupy it absolutely.

Against all Meg's wishing otherwise, they came out of the tunnel into misty, early morning light. Light. The stones were like the fogou except for the window on the back wall. She looked out and saw that they were not underground at all, but instead in an ancient, ivy covered ruin. "Where are we?"

"We're in Ireland," he replied, "in Kilkenny."

"Why?" She would go with him anywhere without question, but this was a curious choice.

Without speaking he led her to a long stone slab cracked and covered with lichens. The carvings had faded with time, but the figure of a man was still clear enough. "This is the tomb of St. Nicholas. The inspiration for Old Saint Nick, Santa Claus, and all the others."

She searched for the crinkles at the corner of his eyes, but he was not smiling.

"I thought he was Greek or something," she said. "What's he doing buried in Ireland?"

"The legend is that two crusaders brought his remains here from where they were buried in Greece. Some people actually believe that St. Nicholas made it here during his travels, so they thought they had a right to claim him."

"Are you one of those people?"

"I am more than that. I am one of those crusaders."

"What?"

"I brought St. Nicholas' bones to Ireland from where they rested in the Cathedral at Myra, because I had a commission to bring relics to Britain."

Meg couldn't accept this story. "You were a crusader? As in the medieval crusades?"

"Yes, but very, very early. I traveled in the service of my king and accomplished his bidding, whatever that was."

"Who was your king?" She braced herself for more of his unbelievable tale.

"King Arthur."

"A knight of King Arthur? As in the Round Table and the Holy Grail King Arthur?"

"Yes. Hidden in the mists of history, the stories are true."

"You are asking me to believe that you are a thousand years old? You do realize that is completely incredible." She loved him, and she wanted desperately for him to be everything he seemed, but this was more than she could accept.

"I understand that, but I want you to know the truth. You more than anyone else." He paused, and then he pressed on with his story, ignoring her doubts. "Wherever we passed through as we came home, children were attracted to us like flies to honey. They chased us until we stopped to speak with them. Gareth, who was my brother and companion, and I felt we had to give them something, so we dropped coins into their little hands. They were so excited you would think we had given them an entire bag of gold. At first we thought boldly that they were attracted by our impressive appearance as knights, but then we realized they should be afraid of us in our armor and swords. Instead, they always followed the horse that carried the relics, dancing and laughing. They moved me in a way I had never been moved before. When on my adventures I found the fogou and its secrets, I saw a chance to carry on his mission, to serve the unserved."

"The unserved?"

"Children. Nicholas is the patron saint of children, and I saw for myself how they were drawn to him. I took his name and adopted his quest as my own."

"How is this possible?"

"I told you that I'm older than I look."

"I can buy older, but come on, King Arthur? At best you should be one of those ghosts I felt haunting Tintagel."

"I am a man like any other man."

"Not exactly like any other man."

"Do I look like a thousand year old man? Do I feel like a ghost?"

Of course he didn't feel like a ghost. That was why she couldn't accept this revelation. His breath tickled her neck, his arms flexed and relaxed when he lifted her on and off the horse. His body pushed against hers when he held her close and they breathed together, and his heart beat against her hand on his chest. This was a man made of flesh and blood, a heartbreakingly handsome, virile human man with expressive blue eyes and a deep, soothing voice. Still, he had to be a man who was playing a joke on her. Perhaps this was another of his tests.

"Nick, please," she pleaded. "No games this time." Panic squeezed her chest and caused her heart to beat erratically. She had the terrible feeling her bubble of happiness was about to burst.

What should I do? Desperation tightened her chest. What should I do? Should I call his bluff? Run away? Should I scream and yell until he tells me the truth?

Finally she did the only thing that made any sense to her. She threw her arms around his neck and pulled him down into a deep, passionate kiss. Caught off-guard, his body went rigid in her embrace, but she did not surrender. She pressed the kiss until he relaxed and responded.

Nick, who was always so calm and composed, was stunned speechless. When he finally found his voice it was hardly more than a whisper. "What was that for?"

"It was for 'I love you', Nick," she responded automatically. "Whoever you are, wherever you've been, whatever you've done—I love you, and I don't care about anything else."

"You'll be giving up a lot to stay with me," he insisted.

"Not so much," she replied. "You've seen my life, my family. I love them, but they will be fine without me. They've managed for nearly a year already. It's almost as though fate was setting me up to be with you. And anyway," she continued, "you said I can see them from time-to-time."

"Yes. But I don't want you to jump to a rash decision. For whatever reason, we do not age while we are in our village. It is just a matter of time before they notice that you are not getting older. Your nephews will grow into men until they seem to be roughly your same age, then as they continue through their lives you will seem younger. And we can never bring your family there. If we are discovered all the good we can do will become impossible."

Things did feel different, special, and even magical there, but that was not something that she could quantify. She forced herself to approach her decision like Dan approached his legal cases. Facts.

Fact: Nick appeared and disappeared like a phantom. He was real and solid, a real man who appeared and disappeared like a ghost.

Fact: They travelled across great distances at impossible speeds, though she never felt that she was doing more than riding a fast horse. A fast horse from wherever they are to the United States? What about the ocean in between? Never mind the time. It takes seven hours to go from the US to London by *airplane*. Anything on the ground, like a ship, should take way longer. Days. It took them a couple of hours, if that.

Fact: Nick had been right about every situation where he had put her. She found the people where he said they would be, and every scheme he set up worked without a hitch.

Fact: The situations had all been in different places in the country with people who had no awareness of each other or direct connection to Nick. They all required that she quickly enter and leave someone's life without arousing suspicion about her motives, and Nick arranged that flawlessly every time.

But King Arthur? No way.

"Okay," she said. "I admit that I am struggling a bit with the time warp. If what you say is true, then all the other people who live in your village…"

"Found the fogou and came at different times, deciding to stay for their own reasons."

"Did you kidnap them all like you did me?"

He chuckled. "No, only you."

"Why was I so lucky?"

"Because you were about to go over that cliff. I saved you the first time and distracted you for a while, but you were going to go over another one sometime, somewhere. I had to stop that." He tipped her chin up to look in her eyes and kissed her.

When they broke apart he said in a low husky voice, "Knowing all of this, will you stay with me?"

"It took you long enough to ask," she replied and sealed her acceptance with another kiss. This was her true gift, the best Christmas gift of all.

Nick.

The End

About the Author

Beth Warstadt has ancient (1981) Bachelor's and Master's degrees in English from Emory University. She has seen two books to publication: *Soul Lost* available for Amazon Kindle; and *Megan's Christmas Knight* published by Gilded Dragonfly Books. All of her stories are set in the real world but contain romantic and fantastic elements applicable to a variety of genres.

Her non-writing persona is primarily defined by being a wife and mother. She has two grown sons. In her time she has been room mom, baseball mom, soccer mom, hockey mom, band mom, and football mom, and she spent seven years coaching elementary school teams for Odyssey of the Mind. She is a southerner, born and bred in Nashville, Tennessee, and currently resides with her husband in a small-town suburb of Atlanta called Suwanee.

Connect with Beth Warstadt on Facebook

https://www.facebook.com/beth.warstadt?fref=ts

More from Gilded Dragonfly Books

Anthologies:

A Stone Mountain Christmas

Haunting Tales of Spirit Lake

Finding Love's Magic

Legends of the Dragon

Carousel Déjà Vu

Novels

Atterwald

Shaman Woman

The Extraordinary Adventures of Ultra-Chick and Rabid Wolf

Crimson Dreams

The Extraordinary Adventures of Ultra-Chick and The Threat from Below

Cheerleader Dad

A Little Christmas Magic

When It's Love, I'll Let You Know

Matt's Christmas Angel

Lila, My Love

Connect with Gilded Dragonfly Books

www.gildeddragonflybooks.com

https://www.facebook.com/GildedDragonflyBooks/